Other Titles by TW Brown

The DEAD Series:

DEAD: The Ugly Beginning
DEAD: Revelations
DEAD: Fortunes & Failures
DEAD: Winter
DEAD: Siege & Survival
DEAD: Confrontation
DEAD: Reborn
DEAD: Darkness Before Dawn
DEAD: Spring
DEAD: Reclamation
DEAD: Blood & Betrayal
DEAD: End

NEW DEAD Series:
DEAD: Onset (Book 1 of the New DEAD Series)
DEAD: Alone (Book 2 of the New DEAD Series)
DEAD: Suffer the Children (Book 3 of the New DEAD Series) Sept 2017

DEAD: Snapshot— {Insert Town Here}

*DEAD: Snapshot—**Portland, Oregon***
*DEAD: Snapshot—**Leeds, England***
*DEAD: Snapshot—**Liberty, South Carolina***
*DEAD: Snapshot—**Las Vegas, Nevada*** (August 2017)
*DEAD: Snapshot—**Estacada, Oregon*** (September 2017)
*DEAD: Snapshot—**Tokyo, Japan*** (2018)

That Ghoul Ava

That Ghoul Ava: Her First Adventures
That Ghoul Ava & The Queen of the Zombies
That Ghoul Ava Kick Some Faerie A**
Next, on a very special That Ghoul Ava
That Ghoul Ava…on the Lam!
That Ghoul Ava On a Roll
That Ghoul Ava Sacks a Quarterback

You can find my titles
in audio format as well.

Audible.com

That Ghoul Ava

Finds an *Appetite for Deception*

(The *Scooby Doo* episode.)

TW Brown

authortwbrown.com

Estacada, Oregon, USA

That Ghoul Ava Finds an *Appetite for Deception*
©*2017 May December Publications LLC*

Printed in the U.S.A.

ISBN 978-1-940734-59-0

For the REAL members of
Appetite for Deception

The World's Greatest
Guns-N-Roses Tribute Band!

A moment with the author…

For a story that started as a short thank you gift for one of my earliest fans, That Ghoul Ava has grown into something incredible. I can't believe that this year could be the debut of this series in graphic novel form.

I won't take much of your time here, but I do want to take just a moment to thank you all for coming along on this journey. Ava is my "break" from the world of zombies. I love Ava, and hope she continues for many more adventures.

I do want to take a moment to thank the Tribute Band community here in the Portland, Oregon area for their support, friendship, and amazing entertainment value. This story is a thank you to all of you, but it does feature the band *Appetite for Deception*—The World's Greatest Guns-N-Roses Tribute Band. Seriously, check them out on YouTube and see for yourself.

To the members of *Appetite*: Michael Killian, Brandon Cook, Wade Sardanko, Andrew Greene and Mark Thomas, you guys are truly rock stars. Thanks for playing along. To Caroline Harmon, the official President of the That Ghoul Ava fan club, you are a wonderful friend and Ava is lucky to have you in her corner. To my Beta readers: Heather, Justin, Nancy, Shelly, Nita, and Cynthia, you are absolutely invaluable. This book would not be in fighting shape without you. As always, to my wife Denise, I couldn't do any of this without your love and support.

I will step aside now and let you get to what you came for, but I still have to make that last plea for reviews. Good or bad, they are the metric that Amazon uses to put this book in front of readers who might not now Ava exists. And yes, I read them all, so consider it a note to me just telling me how you felt.

"Do you know where you are…"
TW Brown
February 2017

Contents

1

Rock This Town

The screaming and wailing drowned out everything as they rose in pitch and intensity. There was a blinding flash of red that seemed to strobe in time with the thunderous crashing noises. A cacophony of sounds fought each other and climaxed with one final and piercing yell that the man let loose with while the people around me watched as if hypnotized.

Then…a single second of silence when it all came to an abrupt end, accompanied by utter blackness that plunged the nearby humans around me into temporary blindness. A moment later, the dirty glow of lights illuminated the cavernous room and people began milling away, all of them speaking much too loudly as their hearing had not yet healed from the last seventy minutes of the high-decibel assault perpetrated on them.

I turned to Kari—an elf, and the regional Psychic of the Dallas area—who was in town to meet up with Morgan and a few other Psychics. They were heading out of town tomorrow for some big meeting in London. Apparently there are more than a few Psychics that want to at least give Morgan the appearance that they will be on our side when the fighting starts.

"That was amazing!" I gushed. "I would've never taken you for a Guns-N-Roses fan."

"Why? Because I am an elf?" she sniffed.

"No…it's just…I guess I just pictured you dancing to the songs of nature or something."

"You really need to stop watching those movies," Kari said, peering down at me over her dark sunglasses despite the fact that I was taller. I don't know how she managed to pull it off, but I was willing to bet she could look down at me even if I was on the roof and she was lying in the ground.

"Snobbish elf," I muttered.

"Uneducated ghoul," she shot back.

We both made eye contact and then laughed like a pair of girlfriends out for a night of fun. Oddly enough, that was exactly what we were at the moment. She'd actually come to my new home to invite me out this evening. At first I thought her arrival was merely to inspect the work done on the elven keep that I now called home. When she asked me to go out that night, I waited for her to tell me what job or mission she would be hiring me to do. Only…she never asked. It was just a night out.

I was about to start for the door when I noticed the singer for *Appetite for Deception* step out from the curtained off area where the big security guard stood posted up with his massive arms folded across his expansive chest. Almost immediately, there was a rush of a dozen or so fans asking him to pose for pictures.

"Now there's something you probably wouldn't catch the actual Guns-N-Roses doing without it costing a few hundred bucks," I said with a wry smile.

"It's one of the remarkable things about this scene," a voice said from just to my left.

I turned to see a rather short, balding man with glasses standing there. He glanced up at me and gave a smile that was so warm and friendly I would have sworn that we were old buddies and that perhaps I'd simply forgotten his name.

"My name's Dwight," the man said by way of introduction.

Okay, scratch that, I thought. I was almost positive that I didn't know anybody named Dwight, plus, he was introducing himself. That would indicate that he didn't know me either.

"Kari," the elf replied, giving me a not-too-gentle elbow in the ribs. "My rude friend here is Ava."

Dwight laughed and then nodded past us back to where the people had gathered around what was now a pair of band members. "The tribute bands are really good about coming out after the show to meet the audience."

"There are other cover bands doing this kind of thing?" I asked, glancing back just in time to see the singer signing some woman's partially exposed breast who looked like her forties were vanishing in the rearview mirror. I turned back to Dwight. "These people do know that those aren't the real Guns-N-Roses, right?"

"Pretty much, but a band as good as Appetite usually gets people to forget. They sort of take people back in time to maybe when they saw them in high school or college. For some of us who never got to see the real thing, this is as close as it gets." Just then, Dwight looked past me and waved.

I looked back again to see the lead guitarist and bass player emerge. The one made to look like Slash was heading our way. For some stupid reason, I got a silly tingle in my mommy parts as he strolled up and clapped Dwight on the shoulder, then looked over at me. "How'd we do tonight?" the man asked with a soft-spoken voice that did not match the rough and ready persona that I'd been watching on stage.

"Umm...good." I winced inwardly as my voice cracked just a little.

"You guys were amazing as always," Dwight added.

I shot a look at the man who now seemed even shorter now that he was standing beside the guitarist. There was not the slightest indication that he was in the least bit star struck. I glanced over at Kari and noticed that it made one of us. She was looking like she might swoon and be reduced to jelly if the man were to so much as brush against her.

"Thanks, Dwight." The guitarist moved around so that he was beside the man and now gave me and Kari a quick up and down glance. "Who are your friends?"

"This is Ava and Kari."

"And I'm BC Slash."

I accepted his offered handshake as did my elven companion. I guess that the moment had swept me up so fast that I didn't even think about what I was doing. When I saw his eyes widen at my touch I realized that he probably hadn't expected to shake the hand of a ghoul. Being undead, I was at a pretty consistent room temperature. That coolness was no doubt even more apparent after he touched Kari. Elves run about ten degrees warmer than humans, so that would mean about a thirty-degree difference from my hand to hers. To his credit, he didn't say anything. Even more points were scored when he made no attempt to wipe his hands off after the brief introductions.

"You were amazing," Kari gushed.

"Thanks," BC Slash replied with a slight nod and bow.

I was about to chip in with my own hopefully more eloquent appraisal of the show to perhaps override the now lame sounding "umm...good" that I'd blurted a moment ago when I felt an unpleasant tingle in my head. I was about to brush it aside as possibly Boudicca stirring in the confines that Blodwen now maintains inside my mind when I tasted what can only be described as a combination of ash and sulfur.

One of the things that I'd been learning in the crash courses that I was receiving from Mystify was that when an uninvited Supernatural enters Morgan's territory, I get a peculiar sensation that varies according to what has arrived. In addition, many of those sensations are accompanied by a taste. For instance, witches give a tingle like electricity and I taste fresh cut grass.

I felt Kari move closer to me and grab my arm. "Ava," she whispered.

I looked at her and realized she was talking without moving her lips and at a volume that would be no louder than a soft breath to any human ears around. My hearing was such that I could hear her as clear as if she were speaking full volume.

"Something from one of the abyssal planes has arrived." Kari's eyes were wide, and it had nothing to do with the lead guitarist.

4

I could hear the distinct tone of fear in her voice. I just wish she would've been more specific about whatever this new danger might be. I guess she just hasn't been around me enough to realize that I am basically the idiot child of the Supernatural realm. To put it plainly, I had no idea what an abyssal plane was, much less what sort of beastie might emerge from said plane.

I was trying to get a sniff of something that did not smell like humans in their various states of slow—or in some cases, much quicker than realized—dying. Nothing was making itself known. I was still scanning the room when I heard a slight commotion behind me. I turned to see the singer pushing his way through the throng of fans. People were almost pleading with him not to go, but he seemed oblivious as he rather roughly shoved the last few aside.

"Yo, Axl!" BC Slash called, excusing himself from us much more politely than his lead singer was doing.

I glanced over at Dwight who had what could best be described as a perplexed expression on his face. "I take it this isn't just that guy further acting the part by being a dick?" I asked.

"Huh?" The man shook his head and then looked up at me with a frown. "He's one of the nicest guys in the scene. He's always been all about the fans. Maybe he got an emergency phone call or something."

I was betting on the 'or something' part. It just felt like too much of a coincidence for this apparently abnormal behavior to be happening at the same time some sort of Supernatural event was making itself apparent to both me and the elven queen.

My eyes tracked the singer as he made his way to the exit. Twice he shoved aside a fan that approached with a camera extended and a request for a picture. Right on his heels were BC Slash and the bass player that I now recalled being introduced to the audience as Duff McLuvin.

The two bandmates ducked out the door that led to the street. This venue, a Portland gem known as The Crystal Ballroom, is situated pretty close to the heart of downtown Portland. At this hour who knew what might be outside those doors. I doubt even the bravest of your kind would willingly venture outside after sunset if you humans knew some of the creatures that roamed about your towns and cities when darkness falls.

"Are we just going to stand here?" Kari hissed, giving my ribs another prod with her nastily sharp elbows.

"I guess not," I sighed.

Honestly, I'd just really enjoyed a night out that had nothing to do with chasing unruly Supernaturals or dealing with the newly risen male ghoul lurking in my basement complex. No goblins or owlbears…just a night out catching some live music and almost being normal.

I started for the door and felt the pain in my head increase at the same time as that horrid sulfur and ash taste intensified. By the time we stepped outside, it felt like something was trying to use a welding torch to cut its way out from the back of my skull.

"Your highness!" A pair of male elves stepped to us quickly, their eyes trying to watch every direction at once. The pair were like film negatives of each other. Their features and bodies were mirror images, but one was as white as fresh snow and the other an obsidian black that no human pigment could ever come close to duplicating. The black one was speaking while the other continued to scan the surroundings, his hand tucked just inside his tunic where I am sure it was gripping a weapon of some sort.

"Something gated within two human blocks," the guard reported.

"I don't think we need to call them human blocks," I muttered.

Kari shot me a dirty look and then returned her attention to her guard. "Summon my scouts and have them search the neighborhood. I doubt whatever it was would be foolish enough to stick around in the area, but it is still best to be certain."

"How many of your people did you bring with you?" I arched an eyebrow at the elven queen.

"Ava, I know you still do not fully comprehend the severity of the events happening around you, but there is a war about to be fought." Ah, there's the Karidilean Qu'Shen, Queen of the Shamadiel Forest that I remembered. "I will not be a prize won, nor will I be the first casualty."

"I'm aware of what is happening." I did my best not to sound petulant, but I don't think I was very successful. "In case *you* forgot, I seem to be on everybody's list to either kill or try to buy these days."

I had to admit, I'd had some pretty crazy offers. However, for some strange reason, I was apparently going against the old adage of everybody having a price. As hectic as my life had become since I became a ghoul, I'd found some odd form of contentment in my life…or unlife, I guess would be more accurate.

I was about to say so when a brilliant flash lit up the sky from what looked to be just one street over. Faster than the human eye could detect, the two elven guards were at either side of their queen. Me being me, I was already at the corner and peering around it in the hopes that I might see whatever had just caused the spectacle.

"Ava!" Kari scolded. "Are you crazy? Do you have any idea what that might be?"

"Something evil and icky?" I scoffed, glancing over my shoulder before I took off at a jog up the street that, for some strange reason, appeared to be suffering from a localized power failure.

"Good thing I see in the dark so well," I sing-songed. "That means no monsters can sneak up on me."

I was really just hoping that whatever it might be would step into the open and face me. I guess I should have known better.

I passed a narrow alley that cut behind some sort of fancy restaurant and a second-hand store and skidded to a halt. I peered down the alley and was confused at first. My vision in total darkness is as good as a human outside on a sunny day. Yet, for some reason, the end of the alley seemed totally dark. I could not see to the other side and I knew this narrow stretch came out on the adjoining street because I could see the tops of the buildings and the opening if I looked up. There seemed to be what amounted to a ball of darkness that obscured everything just past halfway and about ten feet high.

"Imagine the luck," a voice purred from that darkness.

I took a step into the alley, my hands and feet going switch as Sharkmouth stretched out my mouth and allowed for my razor-sharp teeth to extend and prepare for feasting. I heard warnings coming at me in a rush. They were so jumbled that I could not make out which ones were coming from inside my head and which ones were coming from up the street where I assumed Kari was still hanging back with her bodyguards.

"The ghoul known as Ava...you will make quite a prize," the voice continued. "I will be the envy of all the other demons."

Crap. Not sure if that was said out loud or if I just thought it with a great deal of volume and conviction. I was not in the mood to tangle with a demon. I had very little experience with them, and I hadn't actually fought one directly yet. I had no idea what strengths or weaknesses they might have.

A little help here? I projected inwardly, hoping that Blodwen or Betty might step forward and offer up a solution.

Neither could be counted on for much as of late. There was as big of a battle going on inside my head as there was out here in the real world it seemed.

There are various accounts, but nothing certain, Betty finally spoke up. Her voice was distant like coming from way down a tunnel. *Demons are not known to frequent this plane in their actual form. They must expend a great deal of energy to cross over, and supposedly the trip to cross back into their own plane is even more taxing and must happen at exactly midnight. The slightest difficulty can strand them on this side where, if you believe the reports, they have only a limited time to return or they lose their powers, wither, and die.*

I took another step closer to the darkness and felt an exponential increase in the pain stabbing the back of my skull. Also, that nasty taste was becoming stronger. It was so bad that I expected to see gray if I were to spit.

I could hear a clatter that sounded like a Dumpster being shoved aside and then quickly sprang straight up when one came hurtling out of the inky black. There was a gleeful laugh, but I also heard what sounded like a moan as well as detecting that yummy smell of a human that inched inexorably towards death.

"I will give you this one chance to walk away, ghoul," the voice called to me. "I am feeling generous. Besides, you were not what I came for. If you walk away now, you will be spared."

It has been my experience that when people (or Supernaturals) start bargaining, they are usually starting to worry. If whatever this was truly felt they could take me, they would probably just do it. Of course, I am basing that assumption on what everybody has been telling me when it comes to my supposed value in this coming war.

"I tell ya what," I said as I took another painful step closer. "You release that human and go back to your plane and I will let you live."

The laughter that came out of that darkness was almost as creepy as it was sexy. I hadn't laid eyes on whatever this thing was yet, but I already hated her.

There was a shimmer across the blackness and then that dark orb-like thing popped out of existence revealing what I had to assume was my new foe. If I hated her before, I really hated her now.

Standing in the center of the alley was a woman rocking a Marilyn Monroe body. She had curves that would make guys hurt themselves turning around to watch her pass. Her face was a perfect oval and strikingly similar to Kate Winslet from her *Titanic* days. She had wavy hair that was as jet black as that ball of inky darkness that had obscured my vision just moments before. The only thing off-putting about her at all was the eyes. They were creepy and looked like a goat's with their vertical irises. The color wasn't much better as it was an unflattering reddish-yellow.

Did I mention that she was entirely naked? Yeah. Not a single stitch of clothing, which was another reason to dislike this whatever-it-was as she stood before me in her rather remarkable birthday suit. Her breasts, which were a shade larger than mine, still somehow managed to defy gravity. She had a perfectly shaped triangle between her legs that matched the drapes if you know what I mean.

Oh yeah…and she had wings.

They poked up over her shoulder and looked like they belonged on a giant bat. The tops of each were capped with a nasty looking hook of bone or something that was, if possible, even blacker than her hair.

"So, do I take it that you are refusing my more than generous offer?" the she-demon said as she moved towards me, her hips swaying hypnotically in that simple movement. When she did, I spied a figure lying in a heap on the ground behind her. I instantly recognized it as the singer from *Appetite for Deception*.

"I could ask you the same question," I shot back.

"Oh, you are simply priceless," she squealed, clapping her hands. "I'd heard the stories, but you know how things can be exaggerated. I did not think it possible that you could be as they have described."

"Well, that is where you have me at a disadvantage." I decided to throw out a line and see if she bit. "I haven't heard a thing about you. Are you some kind of bat creature or something?"

In an instant, her face went from strikingly beautiful to hideous as the features twisted, and her mouth drew into an ugly sneer that revealed her vampire-like fangs. A forked tongue flicked and swished like an angry cat's tail. That is also when she turned just enough to reveal…

"Oh, my God!" I snorted. "You have a tail."

It was an ugly thing that looked like knotted rope. It also had what I can best describe as a stegosaurus-looking set of spikes at the end of it.

"You will pay for your insolence," the creature hissed as it took a step towards me.

I noticed in that moment that there was no increase of pain when she advanced. Me being the curious sort, I advanced a tiny step myself and paid for it with renewed pain in my head and an increase of bitterness in my mouth. Okay, important safety tip: let her come to me.

"I have no idea what you're talking about." I retreated and was discouraged to discover that the pain and foul taste did not recede to coincide with my retreat. "I mean, I understand the word you used. Ren used to say it a lot to Stimpy." And if you don't know who Ren and Stimpy are...you have my pity.

"What on this cursed world are you babbling about?"

"Which part was the insolence part? Was it when I asked if you were some sort of bat, or when I laughed at your tail?"

"Stupid ghoul," she hissed. "I am Jillea, the *Pulchra et Crudeles.*"

"What is a poolkra ay crewdaylesa?" I knew I was butchering it. When she said it, there was almost a hint of what sounded like an Italian accent.

"That is my name, you halfwit." The she-demon extended her wings and planted her fists on her hips. "I am a succubus."

"Umm...okay, but what was that other stuff?" I was confused. If you've been along for the ride through all my little adventures, the you know that is nothing new.

"Do you not know even the most basic Latin?" the succubus sniffed derisively.

"I know igpay atinlay. Does that count?"

"By all that is unholy," Jillea swore. "*Pulchra et crudeles* is Latin for beautiful and cruel."

"Oh." I shrugged. "Well, I'm just that ghoul Ava. And I got news for you, Latin is basically a dead language." Okay, I wasn't totally sure about that statement, but it seemed right so I went with it.

"I am going to mount your head on my wall and feed your body to swine. I have no idea how you have built such an outlandish reputation that is obviously a fabrication, but your story ends now."

Before I could react, the succubus threw her hands out at me and launched a crackling ball of energy that caught me square in the chest. I staggered back several steps and felt as if I'd been punched in the heart by Mike Tyson in his prime.

I barely had time to recover when the demon launched herself at me. Her hands, which looked perfectly normal just a moment ago, were now vicious claws. I barely had time to duck and still caught one across my face. The stinging sensation was like molten lead had been poured into each furrow and I could not hold back a little shriek of pain.

"Seriously, where did those stories come from?" the succubus taunted as she crouched and prepared to fly at me again.

When she came, I was a little bit more prepared and side-stepped her attack while bringing my own claws into play. I felt them connect with something and heard what sounded like wet paper being ripped. Now it was the succubus' turn to howl in pain.

"The stories are all true, sister," I shot back. "And they are all available in paperback, eBook, and audio versions." (See what I did there?)

"I take back what I said about feeding you to swine," Jillea growled. "I am going to devour you myself so that I may have the pleasure of defecating you."

"That's nasty," I said with a scowl. "And not something that should be spoke of in polite company. Wow, I guess manners are something you might want to brush up on." I paused for just a slightly dramatic effect. "Oh yeah, I'm going to put an end to you. So I guess it's a moot point."

I gave myself a mental pat on the back for using the word 'moot' in a sentence. I think the first time I ever heard that word was in the Rick Springfield song, *Jessie's Girl*. That might've also been the first time a song made me open a dictionary.

We circled each other and I found that, as long as I did not make the move to advance, the pain and terrible taste did not grow any stronger. That was a huge disadvantage. I could not initiate an attack without suffering. All of my attacks had to come when she made moves toward me. I did notice that her left wing was drooping considerably and guessed that to be where I'd scored my first hit on her.

After we circled to the left and then to the right a few times, I got antsy and made a lunge. The sudden and massive pain in my skull threw off my aim and I swished at empty air. To make it worse, the succubus leapt high into the air and raked me with the talons that sprung from her feet. It sort of reminded me of my own switch digits. I was certain that I would've noticed them if they'd been there before.

"Why do you care about this human?" the succubus asked, casting a glance over her shoulder.

I stopped moving and regarded her for a moment. That wasn't a terrible question. It wasn't like I knew they guy. He was just some mortal. Sure, he had a striking resemblance to the actual singer of Guns-N-Roses, but why would that have me out here risking my behind?

"Because he lives in this district," I answered simply. "Anything that lives here in this district is under my protection."

"Lies," the succubus shot back. "Ghouls are not protectors, they are killers. Pure and simple."

That wasn't the first time I'd heard that sort of thing. And I'd certainly done my share of killing lately. Still, that didn't mean that I enjoyed it. It wasn't what or who I was no matter what the stories say.

"This is your last warning." I took a step back from her. I wanted the wall of one of the buildings at my back. That would hopefully keep her on the ground if she chose to attack me again.

The demon laughed, but I noticed that her eyes were just a bit pinched. I was hoping that it was due to the hit I'd scored on her wing. I expected her to come at me, and I saw her tense as if she was about to, but then she stopped suddenly and cocked her head.

"I have what I need," she snarled. "Be fortunate that you do not face me alone."

There was a pop and a crackle and the smell of ozone mixed heavily with that of sulfur. In a flash of black, she was gone.

That Ghoul Ava Finds an *Appetite for Deception*

2

Night Songs

I looked around, but the pain in my head was already receding—not vanishing entirely, but it was down to a level that I could ignore. The taste and smell were completely gone.

"Ava!" Kari cried, sounding equal parts relieved and angry. "What were you thinking going off after a demon by yourself? Now is not the time for heroics. We need you now more than ever."

The elven queen and her host of protectors jogged up to me. There were now six bodyguards instead of just the two I'd seen a moment ago when we exited the Crystal Ballroom. I noticed that none of the elven fighters allowed her to get any farther than within arm's reach of me. Also, they were looking everywhere, searching for any sign of danger.

"What do you know about succubuses...or is it succubi?" I shook my head to dismiss a thought that was unimportant at the moment.

"Succubi are female demons that thrive on draining males through sexual intercourse," Kari explained. "Was that what arrived?"

"That's what she claimed to be," I said with a shrug.

"Where is she?" Kari looked past me with a curious expression.

"She vanished. I think she had her sights set on the singer from *Appetite for Deception*." I turned to where the man had been curled up on the ground. There was no sign of him. I hadn't seen Jillea grab him, and he had certainly not been in any condition to get up and walk away.

"She gated." Kari stepped up beside me. "But she could not have returned to her plane. Not so soon after breaking into ours. They simply are not strong enough. In fact, as far as demons are concerned, they are really quite minor. Also, it is well past midnight. She must gate home at the stroke of twelve."

"Or she turns into a pumpkin?" I asked hopefully.

I considered the pain she'd inflicted on me and decided that, if she was only a minor demon, I never wanted to tangle with one of the bigger types. She'd also mentioned that my reputation was known in whatever plane or world she came from. I was not liking that in the least. Unfortunately, there were more pressing matters.

"She took the singer," I said.

"Then his being is forfeit," Kari said without even the slightest indication that it was an undesirable thing. She could've just as easily been telling me that the sun would come up tomorrow.

"What do you mean by his being is forfeit?" I pressed.

"I mean that, for whatever reason, this particular succubus has chosen her next plaything. She will gate back to her home as soon as she has the power. Once there, she will slowly drain his life from him through sex. Eventually he will die and she will have consumed his essence. I assure you, he will not be suffering. Succubi are very good at one thing…pleasure."

"But he is going to die. You say that like it means nothing." I had a feeling I knew what her response was going to be.

"He is human. He is of no consequence."

Nailed it.

"I don't care where you place humans in the scheme of things down in Dallas, but here, things are different. This person does not deserve to have his soul drained no matter how much fun he might have in the process," I argued.

"I forget that you are still not that far removed from your humanity." She was back to being Queen Kari. I guess our fun lady's night out was done. "Do not concern yourself, Ava. This has been the way of things for longer than even your dear Morgan has been around."

"Just because it is the way things have always been does not make it right." I was starting to get angry. "I am not going to just sit back and do nothing. You say she has to recharge or whatever before she can go back to wherever it is she comes from. That means there is still time to save him."

"Save who?"

I turned to see BC Slash and Duff McLuvin come around the corner and stop at the end of the alley. Both looked like they were almost out of breath. Duff was holding his cell phone and staring intently at the screen with a look of confusion.

I didn't know what to say. There are very strict rules about informing humans about the Supernaturals.

"You haven't seen Axl M, have you?" BC Slash asked. "Duff says that his phone was in this direction, but that it suddenly vanished."

"You track his phone?" I asked, since I didn't really have a satisfactory answer to their question at the moment.

"There were some strange threats a few weeks ago and he was worried that it might be some crazy fan," Duff explained.

"I don't think it helped any that we were all pretty drunk and watching that movie *Misery* with that crazy fan lady," BC Slash added with a peculiar happiness.

It did not go unnoticed by me that Duff gave just the slightest eye roll when his bandmate spoke. I was starting to form a picture in my head.

"Do you think that is connected to this evening?" I asked.

Duff opened his mouth, but BC spoke first. "No, we watched that movie a few weeks ago."

And there it was again. I was pretty sure I'd seen that same expression before. The significant difference was that it was usually when I was speaking.

"I wouldn't rule it out," Duff said flatly, obviously trying to pretend that his cohort had not spoken. "This sort of thing happens every once in a while."

"But something made you take this one a bit more serious?"

"I didn't hear the actual call, but whatever was said made Axl M more than a little bit nervous."

"Ava, I think we need to go." I heard Kari speaking, and that tone was the one I imagine that she used when she was addressing her subjects. It was not a request. It was a command. The problem with that was that I wasn't one of her subjects.

"I think I might have a line on your friend," I said to Duff, pretending that I hadn't heard her royal eflness. "But I can't make any promises."

"Are you some sort of private investigator?" Duff asked.

"Something like that," I replied.

"Are you undercover right now?" BC asked.

"Umm, no. Why do you ask?"

"Your costume." The guitarist pointed at me with a smile that was as charming as it was naïve.

If I had a heartbeat or blood pressure, it would've gone through the roof at that exact moment. I shot a glance over at Kari who now wore an expression that combined disapproval with a hint of I-told-you-so sarcasm.

My gray flesh tone was not a problem on its own. Most people would discount it as some sort of skin condition and would not ask for fear of embarrassment. Unfortunately, in all the excitement, I'd completely forgotten that I'd gone full ghoul. My finger and toe switch-digits were still extended and I still had Sharkmouth. I had obviously lost my normal shades in the scuffle because I did not feel them on my face. That meant that my solid black eyes were on display as well. Like my skin, those could usually be explained away as contacts. But with all of this at once…I was toast.

"Hey, fellas. We were looking everywhere for you. What are you doing here?" another voice called.

As one, Kari's entire contingent spun. I saw them start to

reach for what I assumed were their weapons. Just as fast, and probably not even noticed by the humans, they relaxed and brought their hands back to their sides.

The drummer and other guitarist strolled into the alley, each of them holding what looked like a large take-out box. My nose picked up on a peculiar mix of smells that could not be coming solely from those boxes. I got hints of vinegar, garlic...and chocolate?

"Axl M seems to be missing," Duff turned and addressed his friends.

"Probably took off with some girl. If we kept all the panties thrown up on the stage, we could open a lingerie store," the drummer snorted.

"I doubt his wife would approve," Duff said sternly.

"Oh...yeah." The guitarist looked around with a confused expression. "I thought she stayed home tonight."

"She did, Izzy." Duff's voice was beginning to sound a lot like Morgan after one of our lengthy talks.

I suddenly felt terrible for Morgan. If this was how our neetings went then I was going to have to try and do something to change it. I wasn't exactly sure what but maybe I could start by paying attention at least half the time when she was talking.

"Then why would he take off with some girl?" Izzy pressed as his eyes went down to the box he was holding. I couldn't be sure, but I believe I saw the slightest hint of drool forming in the corners of his mouth.

"He wouldn't."

I didn't see how the other three weren't picking up on Duff's exasperation. If I was hearing it then it had to be really obvious.

"So why would you say it?" Now the drummer was staring at his take-out box as well. It wasn't my imagination, he was actually drooling.

"I didn't...you did," Duff said tightly.

"Oh yeah." The drummer looked up for just a second and then blinked like he'd forgotten I was standing there. "Hey, what's up with the costume."

"She's an undercover detective," BC said happily.

As much as I could've listened to more of this Who's-on-first routine, I was very aware that I only had so much time before the singer was lost for good. If the succubus was able to gate, teleport, or whatever it is that demons do to return to wherever they came from, I was almost certain that there would be nothing that I could do.

I reached in the pocket of my jeans and produced the small silver case where I kept my ID, a few twenties, and the item that I was seeking. A few months ago, Lisa had surprised me with business cards. Of course, they were partially a joke. If a Supernatural needed my services, it was not hard to find me. But I liked the pretty design. There was something about a business card that just felt professional. I plucked one of them from the case and handed it to Duff.

"Call me in a few hours and I will hopefully have some news for you." I turned to Kari and her elven entourage. "Let's go, I need to get to the house and grab a few things. At best, I'm only going to have a few hours before sunrise to get some things done."

I headed out of the alley and towards the parking garage where my Corvette would be waiting. Kari stayed with me until we reached the actual street and then grabbed my arm to stop me.

"This isn't a good idea right now, Ava." At some point, her guards had slipped away silently. That was quite a feat considering my hearing.

"Why not?"

"With me and Morgan leaving first thing in the morning and with Race Mitchell and Lisa Jenkins already gone to their own little meeting to try and drum up more support from the few remaining Templars that are on the fence, I just don't believe that this is an appropriate time for you to be running around by yourself."

I was touched by her apparent concern, but I doubted it was as much for me as it was for this crazy idea all these Supernaturals were starting to cling to about me leading them "into the light" as the prophecies claimed. I didn't even like being at the front of a conga line so, personally, I didn't see the chances of me leading much of anything.

"You worry about your little Psychic Council and let me do what I do."

I had the feeling that part of her reason for wanting to dissuade me from going after the succubus had more to do with how she viewed humans in general. I had news for her, if she wanted to be integrated back into society, then she would need to undergo a serious attitude adjustment.

"Ava, this is a lost cause," Kari insisted. "If she has teleported with him someplace then she has already started the process. Even if you do manage to find him, he isn't going to want to go willingly with you. She will show him pleasures that humans do not even know exist. As a species they are so easy to turn into addicts. Look at how many people voluntarily give themselves over to vampires and serve as blood thralls. They take no account of how they are handing over years of their lives."

Wait, what? That was the first that I'd heard that humans actually became addicted to giving blood to vamps. I had always assumed that it was basically the equivalent of somebody who regularly donates. Heck, there were a few times right after my divorce that I had to go give plasma so that I had enough money for gas to get to and from work that week.

"We aren't going to have this conversation right now, Kari," I said with as much finality in my voice as I could muster. "I am responsible for the goings on in this district. I am Morgan's enforcer and it is my job to deal with unwelcome intruders. This succubus falls under that heading."

"I am certain that she is aware her region has been invaded by an unwelcome entity," Kari tried to argue. "She is likely going to tell you the same thing that I have. This is the natural cycle of things and has been for millennia. One human in the scheme of things is nothing to put yourself in such danger for."

"Tell that to this guy's friends, family, and loved ones," I shot back. I was starting to get angry and doubt my having even considered that it was a good idea to go out with the elven queen. We really hadn't become fast friends in our limited interactions.

We reached my vehicle and I climbed in. It went through all the standard defense protocols—including asking me if the passenger was a welcome guest or potential enemy. Kari did an excellent job of hiding her annoyance when I paused for just a bit longer than was probably comfortable for her before giving my answer.

The drive out to my fortress home was one of silence except for my music. I may or may not have played it just a bit louder than normal.

We pulled up the long driveway and I was surprised to discover several goblins and bugbears waiting inside the garage. When the door began to open, the goblins were able to all scurry out, but the bugbears, being over seven feet tall, had to wait until the garage door was almost completely open.

"Welcome home, Just Ava," Nose Wart announced as I opened my door.

"What's with the welcoming committee?" I asked.

"Morgan is inside waiting for you, and she brought a guest. Your defenses worked as they are supposed to and the new arrival was contained in a holding cell," Nose Wart reported, his words coming so fast that I was almost having a tough time following him.

"She should know better than to bring a stranger to my home without clearing it with me so I can put in the security exception," I muttered as I climbed the steps to my enormous main entrance.

My fortress home was one of the gifts bestowed upon me by Queen Kari during my trip to Dallas where I helped her become the new regional Psychic. I'd also fought a Valkyrie in one-on-one combat as Kari's champion. For services rendered she'd paid me way more than I could've ever thought to ask. I imagine it mostly had to do with how she would've likely been killed if she'd fought the Valkyrie.

"Morgan should know better," Kari sniffed, voicing the very same sentiments that I held at the moment.

I opened the front door and almost collided with Morgan who was standing just inside the main entry. There was a black blob that had ripples that sounded and sort of looked like electricity coursing over it. That was the containment the house's semi-sentient security system had chosen for this particular intruder. Supposedly it tailored the holding cell based on the creature being held.

"Ava, have your security system release Autumn Drueen right away, please," the Psychic said. As always, despite this obviously being a situation that would incite emotions from just about anybody, her features and voice remained as calm as always. The only thing that gave away her distress was her using the word 'please' when she spoke to me.

"Security reset," I called out.

"Reset confirmed," my fortress home security system said in its creepily sexy voice. I hated that my house probably sounded far more alluring than me if you went just off of voice alone.

Kari started past me to approach Morgan and the security system spoke again. "Unauthorized entrance, main door. Elven heritage detected, activating containment protocol."

Again, I probably waited longer than was proper, but I was still a bit miffed at how Kari had switched back to her old self on me. I'd also been doubting her reasons for this impromptu ladies' night out thing. With Morgan standing in my entry with an unknown stranger and the fact that she and Kari were already scheduled to depart for their little gathering, I was becoming more than just a tad bit suspicious.

"Cancel containment," I said just as a gentle hum began to sound that indicated the house was about to enact its magic.

I glanced over at the elven queen and saw a mixture of confusion, concern, and the ever-present irritation. It was easy to guess why she'd been so annoyed just now. Had it not been for Blodwen's counsel, I would've never known that the house was designed with what equated to a computer backdoor concerning the queen and her contingent. Apparently there were a great deal of similarities between elven and faerie magic when it came to their keeps. It had been a very simple thing to remove that backdoor exemption. The only thing wrong was that now Kari was aware.

Later on I would need to ask Blodwen if there might be other ways for her or her people to circumvent my security. It wasn't that I expected to be attacked by her and her elves, it was simply a matter of me wanting to have ultimate say over who could or could not just enter my home freely.

"Ava, I would like to introduce you to Autumn Drueen," Morgan announced, removing my focus from elves and putting it back on this stranger standing in my main entry hall.

I gave the woman an up and down appraisal. She was agonizingly thin and her skin made milk look dark by comparison. She had emerald green hair that I had no doubt was the natural shade and not some dye job. Her breasts were tiny—about the size of tangerines cut in half—and perfectly rounded. That was easy to see through the gauzy gown-like thing she wore draped over her skin that was about as hard to see through as the windshield on my Corvette. What was it with Supernaturals and see-through clothing? Her golden-hued eyes were almond shaped and slightly tilted. Her nose was thin and had just the tiniest upturn at its tip. She reminded me of somebody I hadn't seen in a while.

"Autumn is a siren just returned from birthing a daughter," Morgan announced slowly.

"Did you happen to encounter another siren named Aoife?" I blurted, all my cares and thoughts of rescuing Axl M vanishing in an instant.

"I did, miss." There was a sadness in this siren's voice. I didn't know if it was her normal tone or if it had something to do with her answer to my question. Her next words gave me my answer. "She gave birth to a male child."

Aoife had explained to me the situation with a siren's offspring. It was tied to an ancient witch named Circe who apparently had some sway over the sirens. They all were supposed to return to her island somewhere in the Mediterranean Sea when they were about to give birth. The icky part, and the reason that Aoife hated all witches, was that sirens who gave birth to boys were forced to take them out to the water and drown them. Only females were allowed to live.

"So she had to kill her baby." I didn't realize that I'd spoken those words out loud until Autumn spoke again.

"No, miss, she did not. Instead, she killed four of the witches that were there watching over things and then she escaped. Nobody has seen her since."

"Wait...what?" I stepped up to this tiny thing, the anger in my voice causing all the goblins that had followed me inside to scurry away to parts unknown in my fortress home. I caught my reflection in a mirror and realized that I'd gone full ghoul again...even Sharkmouth.

"That is why she is here, Ava," Morgan stepped up, easing her arm between me and the now quivering siren that looked absolutely terrified. "She will try to sing Aoife home. If we can get her here, then she will be perfectly safe."

I glanced at Morgan with a raised eyebrow.

"Okay, she will be safer," the Psychic corrected.

Yay me. That hadn't been the reason for my look. I was actually curious about the whole bit where this Autumn chick was going to sing Aoife home.

"And how do you sing her home?" I decided to ask, returning my gaze to Autumn.

"Since this is where she now considers home, it is not all that complicated. I simply weave a song of recall together and sing it. It will carry on the breeze, the wings of birds, and even the ripples of light cast by the moon, sun, and stars. It will not stop until it reaches her ears. She will hear it and know that it is safe for her to come home."

"Why didn't she just come here anyway?"

"Oh. Miss, she would not dream of it. She has committed one of the forbidden crimes. That means she is to be executed on sight the moment she sets foot into a region claimed by a Psychic," Autumn said hesitantly. I caught her shooting more than a few concerned glances in Morgan's direction as she spoke.

"I would never hurt Aoife," I explained.

"That is what Morgan said." The siren seemed to almost slump over. I thought that I detected a sense of relief. "I can hardly believe this...but I sense no duplicity in you. Your words ring with truth."

"Ava has a fondness for the siren," Morgan said with an uncharacteristic softness. "There are few that she holds in such esteem, but you can be assured that Aoife is one of those few."

The siren glanced from me to Morgan and a smile began to bloom on her face. It was very slow in coming, but at last it spread from her lips to her eyes. If she was beautiful before, she was simply amazing to behold now. It almost seemed as if she were glowing from the inside out.

After a deep breath, Autumn closed her eyes and began to sing. Having been around Aoife more than once when she wove her magical voice with words that made no sense to me, I was not surprised that none of what Autumn sang made any sense to me.. Yet, I still felt something as I listened. I felt a sense of peace.

I heard the skittering of feet and noticed that the goblins were all returning. None came any closer than to within several feet from the siren. As each of them arrived, they began to cluster together and stare with rapt attention at her.

The goblins weren't the only ones called by her song. One by one, bugbears, the fiery jötunn, and even Queen Kari, along with her entourage, gathered to listen.

I have no idea how long the song lasted. It could have been seconds, minutes, or even an hour that passed when she finished and I came to realize that there was no more music. I glanced over at Autumn and she was still standing exactly where I'd remembered her being when she started singing, so I had to hope that it had only been a few seconds as my mind buzzed with the memory of the earlier events of the evening.

I turned to Morgan but she was, as usual, one step ahead.

"We've had an intrusion in the region," the Psychic announced. Her words snapped any who might still be feeling the effects of the siren's song back to the here and now. "If my senses were correct, it was some form of minor demon."

"It sure didn't seem minor," I grumbled.

Morgan locked eyes with me, so I continued by explaining what had taken place earlier this evening. I could've sworn that I saw her eyebrow twitch just a bit at the revelation that Kari had invited me out.

"This comes at an inconvenient time, Ava," Morgan finally said after I was starting to think she might have been ignoring my little recounting of the incident with Jillea the succubus.

"I wasn't aware that there was a suitable time for demons to start popping in," I quipped.

"Ava, I am leaving shortly. This would be an incredibly troublesome time for you to start off on some journey that you are ill-equipped to handle." Morgan turned and headed into my enormous living room.

This was sort of the center piece of the main floor. The room was easily the size of most people's houses. To put it in perspective, it had four couches set about and one massive wrap-around unit complete with electric reclining ability, seat warmers, individual cup holders, and a pouch for the universal remote that ran the entertainment center. More than once I'd come in this room to discover a gaggle of goblins all crowded around Nose Wart or one of the others that had an uncanny ability when it came to video games. They all thought the zombie games were hilarious and seemed to miss the point that they were supposed to kill them instead of offering themselves up as the next meal.

There was a floor-to-ceiling window that I was very glad I did not have to clean. Not only did it run the length of the room, but it was over thirty feet tall. The windows weren't actual glass. They could rebuff pretty much any assault. Lisa had even gone out with a shotgun and fired it from just a few paces away. There hadn't been so much as a smudge.

"I understand that you are going to some meeting, but are

we really going to allow this demon to abduct a human and take it back to wherever it came from so that she can drain him?" I asked.

"Any other time I would make an effort to reclaim the human, but today is simply not a good day," she replied.

"And so it begins," I griped. When Morgan just stared back at me without uttering a single word, I continued. "We let this one have its way and then our region becomes a feeding ground for anything and everything."

Okay, I was overstating things, but for some reason I just could not let this go. Maybe if I hadn't just watched him perform, perhaps then I would not have cared in the least. The problem was that this demon had done what she did with me right there. I felt it as some sort of challenge. I briefly wondered if maybe these feelings were tied to Boudicca.

"I am leaving Belinda in charge during my absence. I expect you to remain here unless it is an emergency," Morgan said with finality. I felt something tingle in my head.

"Did you just hex me or something?" I snapped.

"I simply gave you a command. Since I have claimed you and you belong to this region, you are bound to obey." She turned on a heel and Kari followed her out of the room. I stomped down to my basement freezer and pulled a corpse from one of the lockers. As I ate, my mind churned over all the events of the evening.

"You aren't so clever, Morgan," I snorted about ten minutes after I heard her and Kari leave for their big meeting.

An idea was forming and I couldn't help but smile.

3

Urgent

The sun was just starting to peek up over the horizon. That meant that I was basically confined to my home. Can we talk here?

One of the things that I have come to despise about the whole Hollywood idea when it comes to films or series about the Supernatural community, you would start to think that maybe it is never daytime. Either that or they cheat by giving vamps a degree of immunity when it comes to sunlight exposure.

"Oh, she is the great ancient Vampire Queen. She can endure the sun because she has grown so powerful."

Blah, blah, blah.

That ain't how it works, kids. Those of us with daylight aversions simply can't go out in the sun. Period. It sucks, but it is the way things are and nothing will change it. I could rub SPF One Million on my skin and I would still be paralyzed with pain if I tried to go outside right now. Oh…and clouds don't do me any favors. The radiation still gets through and fries the undead types like chicken in boiling oil.

As I sat in my light-proof fortress, I focused my energy on the feeling in my head that told me an unwelcome visitor was still in our territory. The slight hint of ash and sulfur in the back of my throat led me to believe that it was still the succubus.

Right now, more than ever, I wished that Lisa was here. She just has a way of finding out stuff about things that I am tasked to fight, capture, or kill. I was still stalking back and forth; my brain trying to make sense of things and formulate any sort of plan when my phone rang.

It always makes me jump when my cell goes off. For one, nobody ever calls me on it. If they do, it is never good.

"Hello?"

"Ava? It's me...Duff?" the voice on the other side announced hesitantly.

"Hey there."

I pulled my cards out and gave them a look. Huh, my cell number is on the bottom of the card. I guess I never really paid attention.

"Any progress on locating Axl?"

I put all my concentration into focusing on the sensation in my head that told me there was an intruder. At some point, I must've closed my eyes, because when I opened them, I was facing in a different direction.

"I got a general idea." Hey, that was the truth. Vague...but true.

"Is there something about this that maybe I need to know?" Duff prodded. I could tell he had a glimmer of something, but he was very reluctant to accept it.

"Such as?" Since I'm not really allowed to divulge secrets of the Supernaturals and their existence, I couldn't come out and just say, "Yeah, your friend was abducted by a minor demon known as a succubus. She will drain his soul through sex and then discard the soulless corpse when she is done."

"Well, this is gonna sound a bit nuts, but Izzy swears he saw some weird chick with bat wings."

"Maybe there is a convention in town. Don't those comic book types dress up funny and go to those?"

I was greeted by silence. Something told me that this Duff character wasn't buying my line.

"Is that why you were all gray and had claws on your hands

and feet and a mouth full of teeth that looked like they could grind logs down to sawdust?"

Crap. This was not a good thing.

"How about you come out to my pace and we brainstorm a plan to find your friend?" When all else fails, change the subject.

"Actually, I am just pulling up to your driveway."

Had I told him to meet me here in all the chaos? It wouldn't be a surprise if I had and then promptly forgot. I stood in front of a mirror and gave myself a head-to-toe examination. The gray skin might be explainable, but my eyes were two solid black orbs. There was absolutely no chance that I could talk them away. Fortunately, I have dark sunglasses all over my house. Some were put there on purpose, and others...well, they are sorta like a television remote or your car keys. You always set them someplace very specific so that you will remember where they are. Then you spend twenty minutes trying to remember where exactly this amazingly memorable place might be.

I was just shoving a pair on my face when the security system cooed, "We have detected the presence of humans on the entry step." There was a pause, then, "Shall we exterminate it?"

What really creeped me out about the voice my home security spoke with was that her dialog was audible sex. It was the Leg Lamp of voices. (That was a reference to *A Christmas Story*, and if you have never seen that little holiday gem...you have my pity.)

"No," I snapped as I hurried up the hall.

I reached the door just as a firm rap sounded on the metal door that was supposedly forged by dwarves or some such nonsense. I opened it, being sure to stay back in the hallway so that no sunlight could reach me. I might not start bursting into flames right away, but I knew from experience that the pain was instant and intense.

"I hate to barge in like this," Duff was saying as he stepped into my home. "It's just, there are some things about last night...err...early this morning that I am not able to reconcile."

I stepped back to allow him inside and was shutting the door when I felt it come to a sudden stop. A muffled moan came from

31

the other side, but I couldn't actually stick my head around to see what it was unless I wanted to get scorched by the sun. Fortunately, my hearing dialed in right away and I recognized the voices of the drummer, Sorum, and Izzy, one of the guitarists.

"Zoinks!" Izzy yelped. "I've heard of having the door shut in your face, but this is the first time I think I've really had it happen."

"Sorry, guys," I apologized as I allowed the trio to enter. I continued to hold the door open in case BC Slash was bringing up the rear, but after a few seconds, I had to guess that he hadn't joined his bandmates on this visit.

"Don't believe him," Sorum stage-whispered. "He's had plenty of doors slammed in his face."

The pair stepped past me, and now I got a better look at them without all the excitement of succubi or stage lights to distract me. Sorum was barely taller than me. I guessed him to be about five-foot-seven. He had short blonde hair—unlike the wild mop of blond I'd seen last night—and blue eyes that sparkled with trouble. Being a drummer, I had to imagine that he got a lot of cardio which would explain his slight build. I had to say that, if he weren't he would be a candidate for the "chubby hubby" club. Just as at the show, and then later in the alley, he had food on his person. This time, he was holding a folded over pizza that he took a big bite out of as he took a few cautious steps toward my massive living room.

Izzy was the Tweedledee to Sorum's Tweedledum. Only a few inches taller, he also sported short blond hair, only, his was dyed a sapphire blue which brought out his hazel eyes. On stage, he'd been sporting a funky looking hat and a wig of straight brown hair. He was rock star skinny as well, and also carrying food. His current meal was some sort of massive hoagie with meat spilling out from the edges. I knew there had to at least be mustard on the sandwich considering the dollop of yellow at the corner of his mouth. Unlike Sorum, Izzy also smelled of cigarettes and beer. I did a casual glance at my clock to confirm that it was indeed still well before noon.

The pair ambled off into my living room and were soon yelping out a variety of "Wow! Look at this!" and "How much you think those cost!" exclamations. It was now only me and Duff still in the entry way. At least that was the case until Nose Wart stalked through the archway. He had a rusty blade in one hand and his eyes were narrowed as he inspected our new visitor. Hearing the noises from the living room, he apparently decided that I could handle the situation here and slunk into the where Izzy and Sorum were starting to sound like kids at a fireworks display.

"You were saying?" I prompted Duff.

For some reason, his eyes were drifting around the area where Nose Wart had entered and then exited. There was no way that he was a Supernatural...was there?

"Oh...sorry," he said, his cheeks blushing just a bit.

At close to six feet tall, thin, with brown hair and eyes, he was the least "rock star-ish" of the bunch. The big mane of blond hair I'd seen last night had been a wig just like his fellow band members. Still, Izzy and Sorum had something about them that leaked through. They were exactly what I would expect rockers to be like both on and off stage. Duff was not. If anything, I had a much easier time picturing him in a lab perhaps, or maybe lecturing a science class. He was staggeringly normal. All except for his interest in the general area where Nose Wart had just been. That part was the opposite of normal.

"Is it chilly in here?" he asked.

"Not that I've noticed," I answered, making a sweeping gesture with my arm that indicated for him to lead the way down a hall that would take us to the room that I considered to be my office.

We hadn't gone five steps when one of the side doors leading to who-knew-where opened up and out stepped a bugbear. Duff froze in his tracks, a small squeak managing to make its way out of him...right before he fainted.

"Crap," I hissed.

"Apologies, Mistress Ava," the bugbear growled in his voice that sounded like a grizzly trying to mimic human words.

"I was unaware that there would be any humans present. Shall I dispose of him?"

"By dispose, you mean eat."

The grin that split the face of this massive beast would've made Duff faint if he hadn't done so already. His wicked looking teeth gave my Sharkmouth a run for its money.

"That won't be necessary." I gave a wave of my hand. "But I could use your help to move him into my office."

The seven-foot-tall bugbear scooped up Duff like he was nothing more than an economy-sized package of toilet paper and toted him to my office. I pointed to a sofa against one wall.

"And now I need you to get back downstairs," I said. "Let everybody know that I have human guests for a while and need you all to stay out of sight until this little meeting is over."

The bugbear nodded and headed for the door. As he left, I swore I heard him mutter, "A ghoul having human guests, what is the world coming to?"

I walked over to Duff and patted him on the cheek. When he didn't stir right away, I gave him a firm slap.

"Hey!" He woke with a start and then almost knocked himself out again as he tried to throw himself over the arm of my couch and only managed to smack his head into the wall.

"Just take a deep breath," I said, doing my best to sound reassuring, although I can't say I really quite knew what that should sound like.

"What is going on here?" Duff practically squawked.

His eyes were doing their best to look everywhere at once as well as find the exit. Since I stood between him and the door, he wasn't going anywhere if I didn't allow it. I didn't relish the idea of holding him here against his will, but I needed to get this situation under control. There was a very big rule in the Supernatural community when it came to humans knowing about us. The rule was this: DON'T.

My problem was that this guy had obviously seen things that he could not reconcile. The bugbear had probably been the last straw.

"Why don't you tell me what you think is going on."

I decided to let him do the talking. Morgan had certainly used that trick on me enough. Maybe if he started blathering on about monsters, perhaps he would hear how crazy his story sounded. That was another good thing about humans. They did not believe in the types of creatures that made up the Supernatural community. Sure, there were those on the fringe—and Goths, we can't forget those nuts—that wanted to believe in UFOs, Bigfoot, and Nessie (two of the three I can actually confirm exist), but "regular" folks dismissed us. They considered the believers to be crackpots to point at and ridicule.

"I think I just saw a giant, furry beast that looked like something out of a nightmare," Duff said, his words becoming hesitant as they came. He was now hearing his hypothesis and realizing that it was crazy. He took a deep breath and looked me up and down. "And you're gray. Also, I bet I wouldn't like what I saw if you took those sunglasses off."

"Then we might have a problem," I said simply.

Duff swallowed hard and I almost felt sorry for him. He was saying all the wrong things, and I was bound to a certain set of rules. Sure, I was also supposedly the individual that was going to lead the Supernatural community "into the light" if you believed the prophecies. Unfortunately, now was not the time. Not with some sort of war brewing. It was made worse by the fact that it seemed as if Portland was going to be the frontline of it all.

"Are you going to drink my blood or something?" Duff finally managed to sputter.

"What do you think I am? A vampire?" I made no attempt to hide my disgust. Vampires were nasty. They smelled like chocolate cake frosted in Dumpster filth. Yuck.

"What then?"

"Why are you asking all these questions?" I snarled. "Do you not get the part where you are supposed to shut up and convince yourself that, as old Sergeant Schulz used to say, you know nothing...nuh-THING."

"Are you seriously quoting Hogan's Heroes?" Now he

sounded almost annoyed. "You're some sort of monster, of that I am almost certain."

"For somebody I pegged as the smart one, you're a real dumbass."

"Hey," a voice said from behind me, "did you know you have two humans—" I actually heard the teeth clamp together with an audible click before I turned to see, of all things, Theodore the owlbear standing in the doorway.

An owlbear is just what it sounds like. Imagine an owl's head on the furred and feathered body of a grizzly. The wings both ended in giant claws. Oddly enough, at least in Theo's case, owlbears are relatively passive unless provoked.

"Oh dear," Theodore gulped. "What have I done?"

By the time I turned around, the giant creature was already starting to leak tears from his huge owl eyes. His beak was trembling and his feathers were all lying flat.

"Relax, Theodore," I said softly. "He's already seen too much."

I turned back around to see Duff even paler than his normal ivory skin tone. I was trying to figure out a way to get around having to kill this poor guy when the scrabble and clatter of little feet sounded and several goblins raced into the room. At least he couldn't see them.

"What the hell are those?" Duff gasped.

I'm pretty sure my eyes did that thing that cartoon characters do when they pop out of the head, go wide, and then slam back into place. There was no way he could see goblins. Humans can't see them, pure and simple.

"And what might you be?" Now it was my turn to ask questions.

"Huh?" Duff's head snapped up to me fast enough that I was almost certain he'd just given himself whiplash.

"Since the cat's already out of the bag and you've seen a bugbear, an owlbear, and deduced that I am something besides just a girl with an unfortunate skin condition, I'm just gonna say that you should not be able to see goblins." I shot a withering

36

look over at Nose Wart and his little contingent of floppy eared, so-ugly-they're-cute, wart covered goblin warriors.

"Goblins," Duff breathed. "Really?"

His fear was being supplanted by more than casual curiosity. His eyes had locked onto Nose Wart which I found almost funny considering the fact that Theodore practically filled the doorframe and looked much more dangerous. Granted, he wasn't, but he was ignoring the great white shark and focusing his attention on the piranha in the room.

Very good analogy, Ava, Mysitfy's voice said approvingly in my head.

"Really," I sighed. I so did not want to kill this guy. Sadly, he was not leaving me with much of a choice.

"This is crazy."

"You don't know the half of it."

If he is seeing the goblins, then it is clear he possesses a degree of ability that makes him a candidate to be a Templar, Mystify lectured. *I was actually trying to figure out a way that I could perhaps help you concoct something that would wipe his memory, but he'd seen too much before I could make that suggestion. If he is seeing the goblins, I would simply detain him until Race Mitchell returns, or your companion, Lisa Jenkins.*

Could it be that Duff had some sort of ability? It seemed unlikely, but Mystify would certainly know better than me.

"Listen, I didn't come here to nose into whatever it is that you have going on," Duff said, his eyes not leaving Nose Wart who was now sniffing around the man's feet. Seriously, if he started humping Duff's leg I was going to be very upset. "I just want to find Axl. If you can help, I'll do what it takes, and I promise you won't hear from me again."

"It isn't that simple, Duff." I gave Nose Wart a shooing gesture when he gave Duff's boot an experimental lick. "There is a lot going on that I can't talk about, but the bottom line is that you can't see what you've seen and be allowed to..." I let my sentence fade. I didn't want to say the word, but he wasn't stupid, he knew.

"Is there no other choice?"

37

I closed the door to my office and then leaned against it. "Actually, there is, but it's pretty serious."

I pulled out my phone and scrolled through until I found what I was looking for. I pressed the "CALL" button and waited for an answer.

"Ava?" the voice said at the other end with a mix of confusion and concern.

"Hey, Eileen." I could almost hear her scowl at the use of her name. She'd long since adopted the alias she used on the roller derby circuit: Rock Star Hell. She absolutely hated the use of her real name.

I gave her a brief summary of the past several hours and then waited for her response. I was used to being seen as the idiot child of the Supernatural world, so I braced for a huge ass chewing.

"You say this guy can see your goblins?" Rock Star asked with what sounded like genuine interest.

"Pretty sure." Almost on cue, Nose Wart returned his attention to Duff and started to try and creep around behind the man. Duff's eyes never left the little goblin. "Uh, yeah, he can see Nose Wart."

As soon as I said the name, both the man and the goblin looked up at me. Each had a different expression. (Yeah, I'm actually getting good at reading goblin facial expressions, yay me!) Nose Wart's was one of concern and he immediately backed away from the human and bared his teeth. Duff's was a bemused smile.

"Did you just say the goblin's name is Nose Wart?"

Then the guy did something that would've made my heart skip a beat if it was still beating. He knelt down, turning to face Nose Wart as he did so.

"Yes, and I wouldn't do that if I was you," I warned.

"Is he there right now?" Rock Star asked.

"Yeah, and if he isn't careful, he's gonna get his face torn off," I answered.

Taking the hint, Duff stood up, but I could tell that he did so

38

against his will. He was now at that stage of curiosity that killed most cats.

"Put him on."

It took me a few seconds to process what had just been asked of me. With just a hint of hesitation, I extended the phone to Duff.

For the next several seconds, I puzzled over why I suddenly could not hear the other end of the conversation. With my super hearing, I could literally hear a fly walking on a wall if I focused on it. For some odd reason, everything being said by Rock Star was not coming through. All I was getting were the occasional "uh-huh" and "uh-uh" responses coming from Duff who was standing right in front of me.

At last he handed the phone back to me. I put it my ear just in time to hear it disconnect.

"She will be here by this afternoon," Duff said with what sounded like awe.

"Excuse me?" I gasped.

"She said that she would be coming directly to your home and that you should make the appropriate allowances with your security?"

I was pretty sure he'd meant that as a statement, but it came across as a question. I wasn't about to reveal anything to this human. He was already in deep enough.

"Let's go find your friends," I said, stepping aside and opening the door.

We didn't have to look far. I followed the sound of my home entertainment system. Apparently Sorum and Izzy had not made it past my living room.

We walked in just as the video for *Look What the Cat Dragged In* started. There he was, in all his perfect 80s glory. Brett's face filled my hundred inch, 4k, Ultra HD television. That baby had set me back just over eighty grand, but it was so worth it. To quote Ferris, "If you have the means, I highly suggest it."

"Like, this gal is seriously into Poison," Izzy said by way of a greeting.

He was almost encased in the very soft cushions of one of my couches. He had a bottle of beer in his hand, but I had no idea where it had come from. Nobody in my house actually drinks human beer.

Sorum was stretched out in one of my recliners, what looked like a milk shake resting on his stomach. He gave a smile and a wave before jabbing the straw into his mouth and sucking on it so hard that his cheeks caved in.

"Guys, what are you doing?" Duff asked, the exasperation in his voice giving it a tired sound.

Again I was hit by a tinge of sympathy for Morgan. Could I possibly be this much of a pain in her perfect little neck?

I do hope that is rhetorical, Mystify deadpanned.

"Dig this crazy television," Izzy answered. "Like, who needs movie theaters when you have something like this?"

"All you need is a bucket of popcorn with enough melted butter on it to stop your heart," Sorum chimed in.

"Don't forget the M&Ms!" Izzy crowed.

"Oh yeah...so good when they start to melt. You get that perfect mix of salty and sweet." Sorum had his eyes closed and sounded like he was describing something nearing sexual.

"Guys!" Duff snapped.

Both men turned to face their friend with looks of confusion on their faces. "We'd totally share with you, Duff," Izzy said with a hint of dejection leaking through.

"Do me a favor and go wait for me in the Night Train," Duff said after a few deep breaths to regain his composure.

After a final longing look at my television, the pair headed for the door. I noticed that a bevy of goblins were on their heels including Belly Ulcer. I could still detect the occasional bristling between him and Nose Wart, but I was staying out of it as Butt Pimple had asked.

As soon as I thought of the female goblin, I felt a mixture of sadness and anger. I hadn't realized how much I missed her until she had been basically kidnapped (or goblin-napped if you prefer). Every once in a while, I could get just a tickle of her presence in my mind, but she was sealed away with Boudicca until I could perform the Mindwalk that I'd been cautioned against by pretty much everybody. It seems that nobody has any confidence in my ability to confront the supposed mother of all female ghouls.

"Did you hear anything I just asked?" Duff's voice brought me back around.

"Sorry, no," I admitted.

"I asked you if it really was a monster with bat wings that took Axl, and if so, what kind?"

I pressed my lips together. Granted, Rock Star Hell was on her way, and if there was any chance that Duff might be brought into the Templar, he might be filled in on the details. Unfortunately for him, I could not justify doing that right now.

"You already have too much information," I said.

"So what's a little more? If you're going to kill me, there is no harm in at least telling me what the hell is going on."

He had a good point. It was sort of like my views on things like being late. Whether you are five minutes or five hours late…late is late. Period. The cat was pretty much out of the bag as far as Duff was concerned.

"Axl was taken by a succubus." I let that statement hang in the air for a moment before I continued. "I have until midnight tonight to get him back or she will take him to her plane of existence, and no, I have no actual idea where that is." I'd seen him open his mouth to ask a question and decided to just cut him off at the pass. "She will basically drain his soul or essence or whatever you want to call it through sex."

"You're kidding." I continued to just stare at him until it sunk in that I was not kidding in the slightest. "Okay, so what are you able to do?"

"I have to find her, then I guess I have to kill her unless she willingly gives Axl over to me. And no, I don't see that as even a remote possibility."

"A succubus?" Duff asked, but I could see by the look in his eyes that he was perhaps not as in the dark as I felt. "Like the kind in horror movies? A demon from Hell?"

41

"Not sure if Hell is the right location, but yeah, you seem to have a handle on it."

"So do you need holy water or a priest maybe?"

"What I need is for you to go home and let me do my job. Believe it or not, this is actually what my role in the area is. I am sort of the local enforcer of the rules. I can't bring you with me because I might have to deal with other Supernaturals in the community and they are absolutely not going to be okay with you tagging along."

"Other Supernaturals?" Duff breathed. It wasn't so much that he was asking me a question as perhaps processing the idea that there might be a whole bunch of stuff out there that he'd once considered fiction.

"I will call you as soon as I have something to tell you." I started ushering him towards the door, then, as an afterthought, I added, "And can you write down your number and address so that I know where to send Eileen when she gets here?"

"Who's Eileen?" Duff asked, obviously confused.

"That person you spoke to on the phone that said she would be on her way here and arrive this evening?"

"You mean Rock Star Hell?" Duff corrected.

Crap, she hadn't told him her real name. I hoped that I hadn't just done something bad. Oh well, add it to the list.

4

Somebody's Watching Me

As soon as Duff exited, I ran downstairs. There was a special room that had a golden shrub that had been a gift from Rain, the Godmother of the faeries. It allowed me to call for her. I was going to need her help on this one.

The entire time that Duff had been at my home, I'd been working on trying to narrow down the location where I felt the presence of the succubus. Since she was in this territory uninvited, and I was bound to Morgan, I could actually feel intruders to our region. Having consumed a Psychic, I could also harness some of the powers they possessed which allowed me to get more than just a general direction.

I could locate intruders within about thirty yards. Imagine my surprise when I realized that this succubus was hiding out somewhere in the area of Washington Park. One of these days I would have to ask Betty or perhaps Blodwen if there was something special about that area. That was where Mystify had first approached me. It was also the place where that horrible lamia had set herself up while she preyed on the children of the city.

To say that I had bad memories of Washington Park would be understating things. I saw it as someplace awful. It amazed me that humans loved it so much. Sure, it was pretty, but I can think of lots of pretty things that are lethal.

"Rain, it is I, Ava Birch," I said to the bush just as I'd been instructed. I glanced up at the wall and read what I'd written on a mounted chalkboard. I'd done this when it became clear that I was pissing off the Godmother because I wasn't using some tired old formality. "On the winds that whisper through the forests, I send my plea. If it pleases the Sidhe, I beg for an audience with you, Godmother of the New Noel Forest."

There was a moment of silence, and then the golden shrub began to hum. The buzzing reminded me of flies or mosquitoes, but apparently, according to Blodwen, the bush was singing some sacred song in a register too high for even my ears to pick up. I'd made some crack about it basically being a faerie dog whistle and the ancient gwyll had torn me a new one about my lack of respect. Ever since then, I'd made it a point to try to be more respectful.

The wall behind the bush turned into what could best be described as a wall of fog, and out stepped Rain, Faerie Godmother of the New Noel Forest. In a way, I guess it was sorta cool that the faeries had been so taken by the old Christmas tree farm on my property—which I'd sworn never to harvest—that they'd given it that name.

She was beautiful as always. Her hair was the color of actual rubies, and her skin was taking on a bit of a golden hue that apparently had something to do with her connection to the Sidhe, the magical home of the faeries. She didn't look a day over sixteen, but I had it on good authority that she was close to two hundred years old. Her dress was a shimmering green number that was basically see-through.

As if on cue, a handful of goblins came scampering into the room. Goblins have a thing for faeries and despite it seeming next to impossible to consider, the two species sometimes actually mate in order to bring strange hybrid creatures into the realm.

"Ava Birch, you have called and I have answered," Rain said with a voice that was equal parts sexuality and regality.

I made a low bow as I'd been taught, then took the Godmother's hand and kissed the tip of her thumb. That had been another custom that got me in trouble the first time I'd been told about it. Hey, can I help it if I thought that somebody was messing with me?

"I am honored by your presence and welcome you into my home," I recited.

There was a moment and then it was like we were just two normal people. That was something that always threw me off after so much formality.

"Ava!" Rain squealed and then grabbed me in a hug.

Despite how many times we'd been through this, I could not help but feel just a little bit turned on. Rain was perhaps the sexiest creature I knew—and that was saying a lot considering the elves, sirens, and a few other Supernaturals that I'd encountered over the past couple of years. I had to honestly fight the urge to kiss her every single time she touched me. Katy Perry, eat your heart out.

"Good to see you, Rain," I answered once I was certain I could do so and not have my voice crack like Alfalfa from *The Little Rascals*. And I'm not even gonna say it. There is no way you don't know who I'm talking about.

"Is it true that a succubus has intruded on the region?" the faerie asked, her eyes wide with what looked more like excitement than fear.

"How did you know?"

"The Sidhe has sealed itself and refused to allow any of our males to venture outside for fear of them falling victim to her."

"Well it's true, but she already snatched somebody."

"Really? Who?"

"A human."

"Oh, well then, nothing to worry about." She gave a dismissive wave of her hand and turned to caress the golden leaves of the bush that I'd used to summon her.

"Umm, actually there is a great deal to worry about," I snapped.

One of the things I was constantly being berated for was how I still "acted and thought like a human." Personally, I didn't see it as the handicap that everybody made it out to be.

"Ava," Rain said in a tone that was equal parts condescending and consoling, "the humans are plentiful. Do not be upset over the loss of one…I'm sure they will make more."

"We aren't potato chips," I managed through teeth that were grinding together as I struggled not to absolutely explode with anger.

The Godmother turned to face me, her eyes giving off waves of pity. "Poor Ava, you still consider yourself one of *them*. I do hope that you get over that soon. It really will be for the better."

"And I hope that I never do," I retorted. "And I suggest that you perhaps start considering your own change of heart if you ever hope to be part of that world again."

She recoiled as if I'd just slapped her. Now I had to try and do a bit of behind-smooching. This was not how I'd wanted this encounter to go considering the fact that I needed a favor.

Faeries were great at giving favors. The trick came in what they wanted in return. More often than not it would seem like they were asking for something very simple. In my experience, that was never the case. The only reason that I'd gotten off so easily up until now was because I stayed in their good graces by giving over the section of my property that had once been a Christmas tree farm and vowing never to enter their Sidhe without an invitation.

Since I'd consumed one of the more powerful members of their species when I ate the gwyll Blodwen, I now have direct access to at least this particular faerie stronghold. I hadn't asked but I was fairly certain that theirs was not the only one that I could enter without coming under the wrath of the Heart of the Sidhe which was some hocusy-pocusy sentient entity that kept out all intruders.

"I need to travel through your waygate that gets me to Washington Park's Arboretum," I said as sweetly as possible. "The human that was taken by the succubus is under my protection and I can't allow her to do whatever it is that she-demons do to their male victims."

"Why didn't you say so?" Rain replied. Whether she knew I was giving her a line of bull or not was unimportant. "When do you need to travel through?"

"As soon as the sun sets," I told her.

"Then meet at this spot when it is time. I will prepare a contingent of my guard to escort you from there."

With that, there was a flash of golden light and a gentle breeze. Just like that, Rain was gone. As far as exits go, that had been perhaps her most abrupt. Something told me that I'd really hurt her feelings. Oh well, I could worry about that later. I have enough trouble taking care of one problem at a time.

I glanced at my watch. Sunset was still so long from now. There had to be a way that I could at least get eyes on the demon before I went in after her.

If only Race and/or Lisa were here. They were both unrestricted by such nuisances as sunshine. I was willing to bet that they both knew more about the abilities of a succubus than I would be able to scrounge up in the next several hours.

Do you think that perhaps I could offer anything in the way of assistance? Mystify's voice chimed from somewhere in my mind.

I could certainly use his help, but there was a big issue of trust between him and me. If not for Blodwen, he'd most likely be sealed away like Adrianna, The Queen of the Zombies.

If you think you're confused, try being me. Apparently, one of the big problems with female ghouls, hence the reason that the Templars had once been employed to try and eradicate them from existence, is that we gain abilities from certain Supernaturals that we consume.

What I've recently learned through some of Lisa's research is that nobody actually knows how much power a female ghoul retains or which Supernaturals pass on some (or all) of their powers. Supposedly, that is what makes a female ghoul so terrifying.

We have a male ghoul in the lower levels of my elven keep but I have been told to stay away from him. He seems to be dealing poorly with the transition from what I've been told. He blames me for some reason. Go figure.

What I've been told are the main differences between the male and the female ghoul is that the male only has use of his absorbed power for a short time. In a female, it's rumored to be permanent. All I know is that there are currently as many as seven Supernaturals residing in my head.

Of the bunch, the biggest mystery is the fact that I seem to have the female ghoul that was the main reason that the Templars were created residing in my head. The Supernatural Grimoire has her listed as being destroyed centuries ago. I certainly think I would've recalled having battled and consumed her.

The problem she represents is that she has made it clear she wants to take control of my body and resume her reign of terror. Naturally I have an issue with giving myself over to her. She has demanded that I Mindwalk to face her in my head and do battle in a winner-takes-all sort of thing. I am declining that offer for the time being.

Ava? Mystify spoke up again.

How is it that you are the only one roaming around in my head? I shot back.

Ever since Boudicca had shown up and did who knows what to the other residents, their contact was almost non-existent. Betty did manage to tell me once that she would need a while to recover. The way she described it, Boudicca had attacked them physically despite the fact that they are nothing more than assorted presences in my head. I asked her if they were physical bodies and she said they weren't but that it would be too difficult to explain.

I don't believe she is aware of my presence, Mystify replied. There was a cryptic tone in his voice that caught my attention.

How is that possible?

The same way she seems not to realize that other young man is in here.

Cody? She doesn't know about him? Is it because you are

guys or something? I asked.

That may be. This is all new territory for me. Up until you consumed me and I became conscious of where I now exist, much of what I knew about ghouls was so disjointed. It is so full of contradictions that many scholars in our community only accept the stories of ghouls as mythology twisted with strands of truth.

What I wouldn't give for Blodwen or Betty to chime in right now. I hadn't realized how much I relied on them until they vanished for these long stretches at a time. Considering the lack of trust I had for Mystify, this contact was not doing me any favors.

And are you as dead set against me performing a Mindwalk to confront her as Betty and Blodwen have been? Do you oppose me getting this situation resolved once and for all?

There was a long moment of silence. I was beginning to think that perhaps Mystify either hadn't heard me or that he might be unable to answer for some hinky reason. For the first time since I'd consumed Adrianna and become aware of the presence of her and the others in my head, I missed it. And if I'm even considering the possibility of missing Adrianna then you have to know it's pretty bad. That would make as much sense as you missing a toothache.

I do not believe that to be a wise course of action, Mystify finally answered.

Before I could ask why, the main door that led to the lower levels of my home fortress flew open and Theodore, the owl-bear, entered behind a pack of agitated goblins and a bugbear. I didn't even have a chance to think, *Oh great, what now?*

"The ghoul known as Colt Faber demands to see you," Theodore blurted.

"He demands?"

I'm pretty sure that my eyebrow arched in surprise before I could smooth everything away and act like this was no big deal. After all, that was what Morgan would do right now if she were here. I've been picking up some of her tricks since I've known her. Things like not talking and simply staring at somebody in silence. You'd be surprised at how often others will start talking out of sheer nerves and the uncomfortable feeling of silence.

"Yes," a voice said from the shadows behind the agitated goblins and visibly shaken owlbear.

Before I could say anything, out stepped Colt Faber, former indoor football quarterback and now male ghoul due to a crazy set of circumstances that is explained in the previous adventure. Seriously, how could you pick up the eighth book in a series without reading the previous ones? That's just silly, not to mention a teensy bit offensive to Chantal, my ghost writer who works so hard to transcribe all this nonsense. So, I'll not waste your time, my loyal readers, with trying to encapsulate those events…at least not any more time than I've just wasted going on my little rant.

"Do you ever pay attention to anything other than yourself?" Colt snapped, bringing my focus back and planting it squarely on him.

"I do if it's important," I shot back. He opened his mouth to say something, but I kept going and steamrolled over the top of him before he could utter a single syllable. "You aren't supposed to be up here. Morgan made it very clear to you that there is a great deal for you to learn before you go venturing out in a world that you aren't prepared to encounter."

That had sorta irked me when she'd made that rule. She certainly had done no such thing for me. In fact, she threw me into a fight with a rogue vampire within the first couple of weeks.

"I would consider this important," Colt said, casting a look at the goblins that were all standing around him in a wide semi-circle that put them between us like a protective barrier.

"Yeah, well that's part of the problem." I gave him a dismissive wave. "You have no idea what is important anymore. And until you accept and realize the community that you are a part of is very real and not some drug-induced hallucination, you are less than useless."

"Would some creature called a succubus invading my mind be considered important?"

I couldn't have heard him properly, right?

"Excuse me? You mind repeating that?" I asked.

"I was in my quarters going over some of the pictures that Morgan has insisted that I study when I heard a strange voice in my head," he explained, tapping his temple for emphasis.

I bit my tongue to keep from saying anything. After all, I knew a few things about voices in my head.

"The thing is, it wasn't me just thinking. I let it ramble on for a bit and a lot of it was disjointed. I even tried to answer it. I thought I was going to burst a vein in my head I was thinking so hard. But it was clear that whoever this voice in my head belonged to they couldn't hear me."

"You said a succubus," I prompted. "What made you say that?"

Colt got a puzzled expression on his face, and then he shrugged his shoulders. "I have no idea. That was just something that came to me after a while. I don't even remember when or how, but something in my brain made that bit of information known to me and I don't think it came from the voice."

"Okay. So you don't know why, but you do know that this voice or whatever belongs to a succubus. What else do you know or what are some of the things that the voice in your head was saying?"

"She is planning on getting away as fast as she can with what she keeps calling her 'new prize'," Colt answered with a curious frown on his face. "It makes her feel very good in ways that I'm not comfortable being included in."

I pursed my lips as I thought. It was the first time that Colt and I had been in the same room after his turning into a ghoul where he hadn't thrown himself at me and threatened to kill me. Wouldn't it be a feather in my cap if I could use this situation to bridge the gap between the two of us before Morgan returned?

"Also, I think she has a spy someplace here in your house."

My head snapped up and I regarded Colt with a look of concern. I didn't see how that was possible. This place was an elven keep with all sorts of magic woven into the security. Most of it I didn't even understand but I knew that this place would not let in anybody or anything that meant me harm.

"You're probably just misinterpreting the signal on that one." I gave a dismissive wave.

"Umm, no," he countered.

"What do you mean no?" I instantly felt my annoyance with him spark. "And what exactly makes you so sure?"

"She has a link with something and I was seeing what she was seeing. You were talking to some guy. I couldn't hear what you were actually saying, so I don't know if this succubus creature could or not, but it had her very agitated," Colt answered.

"Wait, you saw me talking to a guy through this link you have to the succubus?"

I looked around the room. I don't know what I was looking for…maybe some huge neon light would start flashing or something. I doubted that it would be a hidden camera, but what could possibly be sending the succubus images of the things taking place in my home? My mind tried to replay the events when I was speaking to Duff, but nothing stood out.

A thought hit me and it was almost a punch in the gut. I scanned the goblins roaming about. Some were sniffing bits of the furniture or licking the walls. Nose Wart was the lone exception. He was standing almost at attention beside the door to the lower levels in anticipation of any order I might give.

"When you got this image…was it like it was coming from up high?" I swallowed hard so I could get out the next few words. "Or from down low?"

Colt seemed to consider it for a moment. He looked like a third grader puzzling over a calculus book, then a light bulb apparently flickered. "Come to think of it, everybody did look awfully tall. And it was the darndest thing. You had this golden glow around you…sorta like the halo images you see on some of the old religious paintings. And the goblins…" He looked around the room and his eyes narrowed. "Some of these little guys were wreathed in black, like a negative halo."

"You wanna run that by me again?"

"I can't explain it any better, and unfortunately, I can't tell one of these guys from the next. I'm not trying to sound racist, but they all look alike to me."

I held back a snort of laughter. "Yeah, well once you've been around them a lot more, a few might start to stick out, but I still can't tell many of them apart."

"Nose Wart?" I called.

"Yes, Just Ava?" In a flash, the little goblin was at my side.

I knelt down and shot a look around the room to be certain that none of the other goblins were paying any attention. "I believe that we have a traitor in our midst."

Faster than I could react, my miniature warlord had his nasty-looking blade drawn and his lips curled back from his teeth in a fierce snarl. "I will gut the rotting nutsack son-of-a whore and force him to consume his own shriveled manhood before I cut his treacherous tongue from his mouth and watch him choke on his own blood."

The sound of another blade clearing its sheath caused me to whip around just as Belly Ulcer's blade came free and the younger goblin crouched and bared his own jagged teeth back at Nose Wart. In an instant, all the goblins present spread out and began to scurry about to form a loose ring around the pair. Somehow, in all the madness, I ended up on the outside of that ring as the line of goblins cut between Nose Wart and me.

"Wait a minute," I started, but Mystify was quick to shut me up.

If you do anything to interfere, you will cost your little friend his clan. If you prevent this battle, it will be seen as you shielding him because he is too weak, Mystify said in a rush.

Maybe I'm protecting Belly Ulcer, I shot back defensively.

Are you?

No, I admitted with an inward sigh. *But I'm not protecting Nose Wart either, I just want all my goblins to live in peace and harmony with each other.* I heard a snicker. *What's so funny?*

When you eventually learn to tell them all apart, I almost feel sorry for you. I heard actual sadness in Mystify's tone. He wasn't being snarky or condescending.

Why is that?

You don't even realize it when a goblin comes up missing

here and there. They have likely had a few dozen fights to the death just this week alone.

No way.

Very much way, Ava. And you should be thankful.

I'm gonna hate myself for asking, but why is that?

Have you seen the sizes of some of the litters? Two mothers this month alone have given birth to litters of sixteen pups.

So, if I was hearing this correctly, goblins kept their population under control by settling all their disagreements with battles to the death. I guess it was like watching all those nature shows. I remember one where this bear cub lost its mother and was going to starve if it didn't get up to speed on how to forage and hunt in a quick hurry. Cut to the scene with the little bear cub lying dead in some bushes where it just ran out of energy and laid down to die. Seriously, one of the cameramen couldn't load it into a truck and take it somewhere? That always bothered me. Even worse are those starving kids' images that run. I can just picture the cameraman holding up a sandwich just out of the picture to make the kid extra sad looking.

While I was ruminating over that heaping pile of sadness, Nose Wart and Belly Ulcer were circling each other in the middle of the makeshift ring that formed in my expansive living room. Strings of creative curses were hurled back and forth, each one punctuated by the classic goblin hock-and-spit. I knew one thing for certain: whichever one of them won this little pissing contest, he was going to be right back in here with a bucket of disinfectant solution and a sponge.

"Show them all that you are the leader of this clan!" a female goblin's shrill cry cut through the room as the two rushed forward with weapons raised for a potential killing blow.

5

Another One Bites the Dust

Belly Ulcer swung high and Nose Wart swung low. Neither of them connected as Nose Wart ducked while his opponent jumped.

I glanced over at the female goblin that had shrieked just before the two charged and was pretty certain that the culprit was none other than Nose Wart's new mate, Teat Mucous. I hadn't cared for her from the moment I met her, and seeing the look of frenzied carnal excitement over her mate and clan chieftain locked in a mortal battle that might not necessarily end well for him did not raise her any in my standings. I also couldn't tell who she was actually cheering for.

You're learning, Ava, Mystify spoke up. *She is cheering for the victor*

Apparently some of that inner monologue had actually been transmitted inside my head. Supposedly my own thoughts were not actually detectable by the residents inside my head unless I wished them to hear. But since when had Mystify started tuning in?

Meaning? I shot back, a bit of anger welling in me at the condescending tone. He might be the only internal resident that I had any regular contact with at the moment but I could just as easily lock him away if he started getting too big for his britches.

She is the current chosen mate of the clan leader. That makes her part of the spoils if her current mate is defeated. For her to openly declare support for one of them would mean her death if she picks incorrectly.

So basically it is a case of ride on the coattails of the winner or die? I don't know why that surprised me.

I got no response and returned all my attention to the fight taking place in my living room. The pair had each scored a few minor slices, as indicated by the blood trickling from a long scratch on Nose Wart's left arm and a divot taken from Belly Ulcer's chin.

Once more the pair circled. Twice, Nose Wart made a feint and then a thrust. Neither of them came close and I saw it as nothing more than wasted energy. A fight in real life is nothing like what Hollywood tries to portray. There is a lot of fatigue with something so physical, and a fight that lasts for any length of time past a minute becomes as much a contest of wills as anything else.

Belly Ulcer taunted Nose Wart with a creative curse slandering the size of his man…err…goblinhood, and Nose Wart replied with one that hinted to the idea that perhaps Belly Ulcer liked little boy goblins more than little (or grown) girl goblins. Neither of them seemed bothered by the insults and again Nose Wart repeated the same feint-and-thrust move. If he wasn't careful, Belly Ulcer was going to figure out how to parry that and turn it against my little buddy.

Okay, so the she goblin can't cheer for a specific side, but can I? I asked hurriedly.

Absolutely not, was Mystify's curt answer. He was about one degree of snootiness away from being locked up, and I was about to ask him to clarify when he continued. *If you openly declare for your champion and he loses, then we would lose the entire clan. The winner would not feel compelled to stay, nor would his honor suffer him the luxury of ignoring your slight. As he would now be the new leader of the clan, they would have no choice but to leave with him.*

I considered that for a moment. Would it be so bad if the goblins left? After all, my main attachment was to Nose Wart. Yet we were about to be drawn into a war. I didn't actually know what that entailed, but I didn't believe I had the luxury of driving away my troops.

Still…if I showed Nose Wart that I believed in him, perhaps that would inspire him to victory. I really did not like the idea of having Belly Ulcer reporting to me every time I needed or summoned the goblins for some task.

Ah screw it.

"C'mon, Nose Wart, you can do this. Stop repeating the same move over and over before you end up getting it turned against you."

There was an instant and sudden silence. I actually took a step back when I realized that the eyes of every single goblin in the room was looking at me. I shot a look first at Nose Wart. I guess I expected a smile or something, but all I got was a blank stare that was on the edge of almost looking annoyed. As for Belly Ulcer, I saw what Mystify meant about the possibility of the younger goblin's response if he won; there would be no way he would stay of his own free will.

The pair continued to circle each other after either shaking off or ignoring my outburst. I felt my jaw start to hurt as I clenched my teeth in anticipation and apprehension of how this would play out. Belly Ulcer made a sudden charge, his blade a blur of motion. The sounds of metal clanking off metal rang in the room as Nose Wart parried most of the attacks. Still, after the exchange, I noticed that he was bleeding from a few more knicks on his forearm, chest, and shoulder.

Why isn't he doing anything? I screamed in my head. There was no response, and I hastily threw up all the locks. If nobody would respond then they could all be locked away.

I shot a nasty glare over at Teat Mucous. She had her grubby little paws clutched under her chin and a look of what I was almost certain to be lust radiating from her face. I noticed a few of the males present beginning to watch more attentively. Unlike Nose Wart's mate, none of them were showing any form of excitement, but they were certainly interested.

Nose Wart swung low and Belly Ulcer danced away nimbly. "Did you come to fight, or are you some bum-buggered little *go-shae?*" he hissed as he threw his arms wide, practically begging Belly Ulcer to gut him and dump his insides on the floor.

I didn't know what that last word meant, but I saw a sudden reaction in Belly Ulcer as well as a few gasps and titters among the goblin spectators. The younger goblin let loose with a scream of rage as he came at Nose Wart in a furious charge. Again the blades clanged and hissed as both goblins unleashed a flurry of attacks while trying to parry the blows of their opponent.

Just as fast as that exchange began, it ended. Both goblins stepped back from each other. I saw at least a dozen new cuts in Nose Wart's flesh. Belly Ulcer just glared, his breath coming in labored, heaving gasps. His arms were hanging limply at his sides, and then I spied a thin line of dark wetness just under his ribs. There was a single moment where I just watched in fascination as that line began to slowly widen into a gash. In a rush of gore, the younger goblin's insides pushed their way out of that open wound, landing on the floor in a wet mass of guts. The intestines unspooled in a rush like a nest of snakes as Belly Ulcer became aware that he'd been mortally wounded. The look on his face almost made me sad. His expression of furious certainty was replaced by one of confusion and then pain mixed with sadness.

Nose Wart stepped forward and grabbed the young goblin by the coarse hair on his head and jerked back so he could slice Belly Ulcer's throat. I wanted to tell him not to, that it would just make a bigger mess, but I figured that this was all part of the ceremony. No sooner had he made the cut, than he also lopped off one of the ears and popped it into his mouth like it was a chip or a cookie. I made the mistake of assuming that he was going to perhaps eat his opponent as a final display of his victory, but instead, he spat the masticated ear onto the corpse and howled at the ceiling.

All the goblins surrounding the battle echoed the howl and

then they all rushed in and began ripping the loser apart. Nose Wart wormed his way out of the throng with something bloody clutched in the hand that had executed the killing blow. If he thought that I was going to partake in their little blood orgy, he was mistaken. For some reason, the meat was giving off a tainted smell that I found almost as unappealing as I did the stink of vampires.

I breathed a sigh of relief when he strode past me and walked up to his mate. He thrust out his hand and she accepted the offering with gusto. As I watched her chow down on Belly Ulcer bits, I could not help but think that she would've been just as happy doing the same thing if Nose Wart had lost.

You must learn to stop judging other creatures by your former human standards, a voice chimed inside my head.

Mystify? I bristled. *I locked you up. What are you doing out?*

You are distracted and the outer locks all fell away, he replied simply. *I do not understand why you do not tie off your spell if you truly wish us to stay locked up.*

What spell?

Do you not realize that you are employing magic when you shut us away? Has nobody explained to you that it is, at its core, a rather simple spell. The degree of sturdiness your lock displays is based on the amount of magic that you employ. But it does not matter how complex your spell is if you do not tie it off. In the end, even the most secure lock will eventually fade given enough time if you do not take such measures.

Even Boudicca?

All locks, Mystify stated simply.

But I don't know magic, I insisted. *I couldn't cast a spell if I tried. At least not on my own.*

I believe that to be true, but this skill is one that is inherent to ghouls...at least that is how it seems now that I have had time to study it from inside.

I didn't like the sound of that. If Mystify was studying me from inside, would he become like Boudicca and eventually turn into another mental resident trying to wrest control of my mind away from me?

And you can teach me this tie thingy? I asked hesitantly.

The last thing I was ready to do was actually trust Mystify on my own. It had been easier to tolerate his existence when I had Blodwen and Betty active in my head. If they didn't come back soon, I was going to Mindwalk despite all the warnings I'd been given.

It is a very simple process, Mystify assured.

Obviously he'd forgotten who he was dealing with. It took three tries but I eventually got the hang of it. When I was at least partially satisfied I returned my attention to what was happening in the room. At some point Nose Wart had dismissed most of the goblins with the exception of those he had stay to help clean up the mess. I did a doubletake when I spotted Teat Mucous in the detail. She was on her knees with a bristled brush and a bucket.

I moseyed over to where Nose Wart stood with his arms folded across his chest. He had done nothing to the wounds and most of them were still dripping blood, but he had a tiny goblin with a rag sitting at his feet that would swipe up any drop that made it to my floor.

"I see you have your mate scrubbing beside the rest," I said casually.

"I believe she wished for me to be defeated, Just Ava," the goblin said coldly.

It was strange hearing such harshness in his tone. While I'd fought alongside him and been in more than a few hairy situations, he still always sounded like he didn't have a care in the world. Right now…he sounded like an angry goblin.

"So does that mean you will take a new mate?" I asked.

"Once I find a female that I believe will be able to displace her in combat, I will taste her and be certain."

I had to puzzle through that statement for a moment, but eventually I understood. If I was guessing right, any female he chose would have to fight Teat Mucous to the death since goblins didn't do things like surrender. None of that would matter until he actually tasted the flesh of his potential mate since goblins eat their mate when they die.

"Any possibilities?" I asked with as much happiness in my voice as I could muster. I didn't like seeing the little guy like this.

"No." And with that single word, he walked away, shouting angry instructions to the unfortunate goblins tasked with cleaning things to his apparently meticulous standards.

Why was everything changing? I moaned inwardly. It was a tension that I could practically taste and it was contagious. As Nose Wart stalked around barking orders like he was commanding troops on the battlefield, Theodore entered the room. He always looked kinda sad, but at this exact moment, he drooped everywhere and looked like I'd just taken away his access to the library.

(Go figure...who knew that owlbears loved to read?)

"The Faerie Godmother has come to your meeting room," Theodore announced glumly. "She demands to see you...and she sounds angry."

I had no idea what might have Rain's panties twisted in a knot but she could just take a number. Also, a foul mood was now trickling into my head, so she was not going to get happy, shiny Ava.

6

Who Can It Be Now

"What do you want?" I snapped as I stormed into the room with the bush.

Rain was standing there surrounded by a heavily armed group of guards that all snapped to the ready-for-battle position when I entered. I ignored them as I stomped up to the tiny faerie. That was when I noticed that her normal attire of see-though material had been replaced by fine chain mesh. She was also carrying a tiny sword at her hip.

"Three of my consorts have been taken, I suspect this succubus has decided to fill her cart while she is here," Rain hissed. "What do you intend to do about it?"

"Wait a minute!" I held up my hands in the universal gesture for 'hold the damn phone'. "Just a little while ago, you were talking about this being the way of things and that it was just one human."

"There are billions of humans infesting this once beautiful planet," Rain exploded. "There are less than a thousand faeries in all the Sidhe combined. I would hope you can tell the difference."

"See, that's part of the problem." I stood over Rain, my hands planted on my hips. "We see things from a very different perspective."

"Does that mean you will not help me? That you will concern yourself with the human while three of my male subjects possibly end up being drained of their being by that demoness?"

"Not at all," I replied. "Since the cases are apparently related, I believe I can handle them at the same time."

Rain opened her mouth and then snapped it shut. Was that how I looked when Morgan put me in check or pointed out what ended up being the obvious?

I was getting a lot of glimpses at things that illustrated how I might look or sound to the Psychic and it was not flattering in the slightest. A small voice in my head said that maybe I was getting wiser or smarter.

(Yeah, I laughed a little bit at that idea too.)

"But you will try to bring my men home?" Rain whispered in a voice that was…wait, was she pleading? Since when did the Godmother beg or plead for anything? Perhaps this was more serious than I was giving credit.

"I will do everything in my power," I promised.

The tiny faerie threw herself at me and wrapped me in a fierce hug. I was a bit uncomfortable with all this blubbering and such. It wasn't that I didn't like a good hug any less than the next girl, but at this very moment I just wanted to try and get my head wrapped around what it was that I had to do.

It took about ten minutes to get the distraught Faerie to go back home. As soon as she did, I went upstairs to discover that Colt had not returned to his quarters.

"Is everything okay?" he asked.

"Why are you here?" I snapped.

Okay, I might be coming off as a bit of a bitch here, so perhaps now is a good time to get you clued in on some of our past. More specifically, I think you need to know what happened in the days and weeks following his waking up to discover that he was a ghoul.

To say that he took it poorly would be a gross understatement. From the first moment that he was told about his situation by Morgan, he blamed me.

After Morgan got Colt to settle down, I made the mistake of thinking that we would be having some sort of meaningful conversation. What I got was him threatening to tear me apart if he ever got his hands on me.

"I'd like to see you try," I shot back.

I guess I made the mistake of not taking him literally, because he launched himself at me. The only reason he missed was because my reflexes were just as sharp, if not sharper. I rolled to the side and came up with my switchdigits at the ready.

He made a series of guttural sounds due to his inability to talk around his own version of Sharkmouth. I don't know why, but that tickled me and I began to laugh at him.

"Ava!" Morgan barked.

That shut me down in a hurry. I'd known the Psychic to do a lot of things, but to have such an outward display of emotion was definitely not one of them.

"He started it," I said, pouting and folding my arms across my body just to give the full effect.

"Step outside," she said, all composed and back to the version of her that I knew. Seriously, a porcelain doll has more facial expression than Morgan.

We stepped out of the room where Colt was being kept and Morgan closed the door. I'd discovered, much to my delight, that rooms in this elven keep were not subject to my superior hearing unless I asked for the security system to allow it. That also meant that other Supernatural beings that might visit would be just as hampered, and they could not ask my security system to override that aspect for them.

"We have a resource here that could be very helpful in the coming months, Ava," Morgan said, obviously addressing the look of curiosity that I wore openly in response to everything going on regarding Colt Faber.

"So he gets to threaten to kill me and I just have to take it?" I shot back.

"Of course not, but he is a bit distraught at the moment, Ava," Morgan replied.

"Oh, and when I turned, did I start threatening people? I

wasn't distraught?"

"I'm not saying you weren't, but Colt is leaving behind a very full and busy life."

"And I was just a waitress, so my life was just a big steaming pile that didn't mean anything?" My anger was in full bloom now.

"You are putting words in my mouth, Ava. I'm not saying that at all, but Colt is leaving behind a wife and new daughter."

My mouth opened and I just stood there like that for several seconds. I'd had no idea. What I did know was that he would never be allowed to see them again. As far as they knew, he was dead. The Supernatural community has a very strict code when it comes to letting mortals know about our existence. In a nutshell, we don't. That was why Duff's life was hanging by a thread at the moment.

"I didn't know," I whispered. I did my best to try and imagine what that had to feel like, but I honestly couldn't.

Since then, we'd been sort of kept apart. I'd gone down a few times to see if maybe he'd gotten over blaming me, but it had been clear each time that he hadn't.

"Is that how you isolate?" Colt's voice made me shake my head and return my attention to him. "What do you think of?"

"Huh?" I was confused. What had I missed?

"When you shut yourself off from external stimuli…although I don't see anything causing you pain. I'm just wondering what you focus on to shut out the world and eliminate your pain," Colt clarified.

"Oh…no. Actually, I've been a bit spacey my whole life. I didn't even know that it would come in handy. Imagine my surprise."

"What do you think about?" His tone had changed and I could tell that he was feeling something deep. My guess was that it had to do with missing his family. I didn't envy him.

"Lots of stuff," I answered. "One time I had the theme from *Raiders of the Lost Ark*…one time it was the *Star Trek* fight theme."

Colt looked confused. "How does that help?"

"No idea. Why, what do you use?"

I hadn't thought that his sad face could get any sadder. I was wrong. "My little girl."

I didn't know what to say to that. I was still trying to figure out something to fill the uncomfortable silence when he climbed onto one of the barstools at the breakfast bar and laid his head down on his folded arms.

"Hey, I know this probably sucks for you, and I'm not even going to pretend to understand what you must be feeling. Honestly, I had no idea that this was going to happen to you when I took the job, and I doubt I could have done anything to change the outcome even if I had."

I was being totally honest. After all, how would I know that he would die during a football game?

"Yeah, I know," he said, his voice muffled from his face being buried in his arms.

That caught me by surprise. It also seemed a bit sudden. I didn't want to push it, but I had to ask. "What made you change your mind?"

"I didn't," he said, sitting up and looking me in the eye. "I was just really mad when Morgan told me that I would never be able to see my family again. I would've blown up at her, but you walked in moments after she'd told me and just seemed like an easier target for my anger. Honestly, I doubt if Morgan would've even flinched if I threatened to kill her."

"I know, right?" I laughed.

"The only time I've ever seen her break that Spock persona was the time she yelled at you that day. Since then, nothing."

"Get used to it."

We sat in silence for a moment and I rummaged through my head for anything else to say. Nothing was making itself available. Part of the blame could be the fact that, gray skin and ebony eyes or not, Colt Faber was simply hunkalicious. Seriously, picture every all-American boy who plays quarterback and I can promise you that they are molded after Colt Faber.

"So, why am I hearing this voice in my head?" Colt finally

asked.

"I honestly don't know, but the fact that you do, and that you can home in on it is huge."

I went on to explain what was going on. To his credit, the guy never even flinched as I talked about demons or how faeries and humans could end up being gated to some other plane to be consumed through sex.

"I guess we have to do something about it then," Colt said simply.

"It's not quite that easy," I cautioned with a shake of my head. "For one, it is daytime and we can't be in the sun."

"Like vampires?" He sounded confused and just a little skeptical.

"No, sunlight is way worse on them than it is us. We just feel like we are being incinerated, they actually explode into a little cloud of glittery dust."

"You're being totally serious," he gasped.

"Yeah." I nodded my head. "I don't know what you've been told yet, but I can assure you that the only reason I'm still in this house is because it is daylight."

"No, I mean about the vampires."

"What about them?" I was confused.

"That they are real."

"Wow, you haven't been told much at all, have you?" Suddenly I was even less jealous of Colt. Sure, he'd gotten some pretty special treatment, but I also realized that there was a whole lot that he wasn't being told.

Since it was daylight and there wasn't much else I could do at the moment, I gave him the condensed version of my exploits thus far. He listened, most of the time with open-mouthed disbelief. By the time I was done, he had a new expression on his face that I didn't understand.

"What's the matter?" I asked, curious as to what might be wrong now.

"You would've probably killed me," he said with a nervous chuckle.

"What?"

"That day I threatened you."

"What about it?"

"If Morgan hadn't stepped in, you probably would've mopped the floor with me. Heck, I might even be living in your head with all those other folks."

I considered his words and tried to decide if he was being modest. He definitely had me in size, but maybe there was little doubt that I had the edge when it came to controlling a ghoul's powers.

"I'm just glad that you don't blame me," I decided to say. "When Morgan told me about your family, I felt horrible."

Once more we lapsed into an uncomfortable silence. We were still sitting there when my home security system broke that silence.

"There is an intruder on the premises. Templar. Shall I terminate?" the sultry voice cooed like she was inviting me to do something naughty.

"Where is this Templar?" I asked, getting to my feet.

"Five yards down the driveway and closing at a steady pace," the voice replied.

"Fast?" I asked, letting my hands go switch.

"Steady."

Was that a yes or a no? A niggling voice in the back of my mind tried to make something register.

"Standby," I finally called out. "Nose Wart?"

There was a scurry of claws on hardwood. "Yes, Just Ava?" The goblin almost seemed to appear out of nowhere.

"We have a Templar approaching, send the bugbears."

"I will lead the charge," the tiny creature announced, and then let loose with a shrill whistle that seemed to echo forever off the walls of my home.

Not five seconds later, a trio of bugbears arrived. Each of them was brandishing massive swords that looked like they weighed a hundred pounds apiece.

"We have an intruder approaching," Nose Wart announced. He looked back at me. "Capture or kill, Just Ava?"

"Capture."

A series of groans and unhappy snorts came from the bug-bears and their big, tufted ears all drooped. Nose Wart remained impassive and simply gave a curt nod.

The foursome turned and scampered to the front door and slammed it behind them. I wanted to watch, but I couldn't even look out a window. I'd learned early on that Ava no likey the sun on her skin.

"One bugbear has perished," the security system announced.

I winced. While I didn't have an attachment to any of the huge creatures, they were still under my care or whatever. I briefly wondered if the leaders of all these countries that liked to go to war so much would be able to stomach it if they had a voice announcing to them every time one of their soldiers died in battle.

"The Templar has been subdued," the voice announced a moment later.

I sighed in relief and waited patiently for Nose Wart to return with the prisoner. I didn't have to wait for long.

The door flew open and a voice bellowed, "You tell that gray-skinned harlot that I'm gonna smack her upside the head!"

Finish What Ya Started

"Eileen!" I practically squealed. Then I was hit by a flush of embarrassment. I'd totally spaced the fact that she was on her way. That had cost one of my bugbears his life.

The gigantic woman gave me an even dirtier look if that were possible. She hated her given name and pretty much everybody called her by her roller derby name of Rockstar Hell...Rock to her friends. I'd already irked her, and now was no time to pull her chain any harder.

"Sorry," I apologized, throwing my hands up in a sign of surrender.

She snorted what might've been an acceptance and then shot a look at the two bugbears still holding onto her arms. They wisely let her go and then stepped out of reach of any sort of attack that might come from the woman who was almost as tall as the furry seven footers.

One of them shot a look over his shoulder at the door. "Go get your brother," I told the beast. Both bugbears took off in a hurry.

Nose Wart remained with a handful of goblins and made no effort to move out of the way of the Templar. She stepped up to him and looked down with an eyebrow raised in question. He simply stared back up at her with no expression.

"You gonna let me in, Nose Wart?" Rock asked politely.

"You are in our home now, Templar," the goblin retorted.

This was not going anything like I might've imagined. Sure, they had not started off on the best of terms when the pair first met during my trip to Texas to deal with a band of Valkyries, but I thought that things ended decently enough. Shocking surprise…I was wrong again.

"I understand that," Rock agreed. If Nose Wart's attitude had me confused, then the degree of calm politeness and even respect being shown to the goblin by this woman who was probably close to ten times his size was even more peculiar.

"I owe you still for that assault in the car," Nose Wart hissed.

"Are we really going to do this now?" I blurted, unable to keep my mouth shut any longer. I was seriously missing Butt Pimple's presence at the moment. I just knew that something was playing out here and she would be able to talk me through it.

"This is between Nose Wart and me, Ava," the Templar said sternly, her eyes not leaving Nose Wart's. "And so what is it that will set us at evens?" When she spoke, she didn't talk to him like she could crush him like a bug under one of her huge booted feet. Instead, she was talking to him like he was a full grown jötunn.

"One blow," Nose Wart replied after almost no hesitation.

"So be it."

I was trying to figure out the logistics of how that would work when my little goblin scaled the woman like one of those American Ninja Warriors goes up that funny wall at the end. Before I could get my mind around that, he reared back and socked her square in the face. Even from where I stood several feet away I could hear the crunch of her nose. More surprising still was when she staggered back a step and almost went to her knees.

Nose Wart jumped down, landing with catlike grace on the floor. Meanwhile, blood was gushing freely from both nostrils and I could see tears leaking from the corners of Rock's eyes. She wasn't crying, but I've been bopped in the nose a few times and know that it will definitely bring on the liquid.

"We are at evens," Nose Wart proclaimed. In a flash, he did a proper about-face and came to rigid attention. "Just Ava, I have assaulted a guest under your protection and in your lair. I am prepared to accept my punishment."

"Huh?" Okay, not the sharpest reply, but I was beyond lost at this point.

"What shall my punishment be for my transgression?" the goblin asked coolly.

You must give him something or he will be seen as unworthy of your respect, the voice of Mystify chimed in my head.

While I was grateful for that bit of information, I didn't want him back out. I thought I'd tied off my spell like he taught me. Apparently I hadn't gotten it right. We would revisit that lesson again later. For now, I wanted him locked away and so I quickly went through the process in about the span of two heartbeats.

"You will stand in silent guard over the fallen body of the slain bugbear for a period of…four hours without speaking, eating or drinking." I wasn't sure if that was satisfactory or not, but it seemed to satisfy the goblin who gave a low bow and then hurried from the room.

"So this is the male ghoul," Rock said appreciatively as she followed me and Colt into the living room. "I haven't seen one of those in years. Not living anyway."

"I'm standing right here," Colt said, a hint of aggravation in his voice.

"Colt, this is Rock," I said by way of introductions.

"What kind of name is Rock?" Colt scoffed.

"I could say the same about Colt," Rock quipped. "Were your parents some sort of New Age weirdos or something?"

In a flash, Colt's switch digits flicked into being and Sharkmouth turned his normally cute mouth into something resembling a wood chipper. From out of nowhere, Rock had a short blade in her hand that looked like something a goblin would use. It was about as dull-looking as any blade I'd ever seen, but I was willing to bet that didn't matter.

I stepped between the two and shot a withering glare at each of them. "Let's take things down a notch," I said with a huff.

To her credit, Rock slid the blade into one of her sleeves and stepped away, her hands going behind her back. Colt also stepped back, but his ghoulish transformation would take a few minutes to revert. It seemed like an eternity ago since I'd had absolutely no control over my own weapons, but I certainly remembered how annoying it was to be at their mercy.

"So what is this about a demon?" Rock asked, turning all her attention to me.

I filled her in on what happened. She listened like I might be sharing a favorite recipe. There was obvious interest, but she wasn't getting all that excited about it.

"And this human that might pose a problem?" she pressed.

I told her about Duff. I explained how he could see the goblins and was figuring things out to the point where it was officially an issue of concern. I'd been told more than once that any human that discovered the truth about our existence—apparently with the exception of vampire thralls for some reason—were made to disappear. Duff certainly fit that category.

"It sounds to me like he might have some sort of sense or link to the Supernatural world. You sure he isn't one of us?" Rock asked after pondering my recounting of things for a moment, pinching her lower lip in deep thought.

"Pretty sure," I said.

"Then I guess we will have to pay this guy a visit."

I glanced at my watch. It was still a good five hours until sunset. That meant that I was confined to quarters. Rock seemed to realize that almost as soon as the words left her mouth.

"How about we have him come here?"

I shrugged. I wasn't too thrilled about the man being killed in my house, but we could deal with that problem when it got here.

I made the call and told Duff his presence was required. After I hung up, I listened as Rock caught me up on all the Templar gossip. It seemed that Race was doing a pretty respectable job at recruiting a decent number of other Templars to his side.

"The real problem is coming from the Council of Psychics," Rock explained. "I guess Morgan is a bit of the black sheep in that circle."

If I'd been drinking something, I would've done the most amazing spit take. I tried to imagine any world where Morgan was the bad seed or trouble maker. I gave up after a few seconds that threatened to hurt my brain.

"She has flown in the face of so many of their edicts that the list is no longer recorded in their disciplinary files," Rock explained after obviously seeing the bewildered look on my face.

"Okay, I'm just gonna go with the idea that you know enough about me to know how little I understand about this Supernatural world. Maybe you can give me one example?"

"I can give you the easiest," Rock said with a low chuckle in her voice that let me know right away I was probably not going to like her example.

"You. That is the easiest one to point out." Rock paused and let that idea fester for a moment. "The moment your existence revealed itself, she should have reported you to the Templars. They would have arrived and disposed of you while you were still in your infancy."

"You mean they would have killed me when I was a baby?" I gasped in horror.

"No, your new incarnation. The day you rose was when you would have been simple to dispatch. At that moment, you had no powers, you would not have known how to use them even a little should your claws and fangs exhibit. Also, your head would've been empty."

I knew a lot of people who think that it still is. Hell, half the time I can't come up with any evidence to contradict that thought.

"Okay, maybe that is a thing, but give me something else," I pressed.

"Sure, she actively engineered placing an ally in power as

the Dallas Psychic."

My mouth opened to say something, but I honestly couldn't think of one single comment. Eventually, one came. "Okay, give me an example that doesn't include me."

"Sure, her chief lieutenant went missing and she refused to name or accept a replacement."

I knew about that one.

"Another."

"There is evidence that she has been enlisting witches for the past ten years. Her territory has at least thirty that we know of."

"What's so bad about that?" I asked, honestly baffled why that would be some sort of major crime.

"The most in any other territory is three."

"Why only three?"

"They are almost as dangerous a ghoul," Rock said with a grim face. "They can delve into various fields, and most territories only have one sort. Morgan has witches in all disciplines." She paused and looked around the room like she expected something to just materialize out of thin air. "Including the four most powerful necromancers in existence."

I pondered that last one. I'd met two of those sorts. Not under Morgan's jurisdiction in either case. The first was that skank Adrianna. If you believe the stories, she was the one responsible for the Black Plague. Then there was the kid, Cody. He'd been in the basement prison of the Dallas Psychic. I'd eliminated both of them, and they both resided in my head. At least I think they both did. Adrianna had been silent for a long time. I'd had her locked away good with help from Betty and Blodwen. Had Morgan sent me into those jobs knowing about each of them and their abilities? Had I been her unknowing assassin?

It did seem to be a bit too much of a coincidence as I started hearing these little indiscretions. Had she hoped that they would submit to me and then come under her control? Funny, but she hadn't suggested any such thing. In fact, she hadn't told me much of anything about any of the jobs she sent me on. And was that why Adrianna had been so determined to kill Morgan?

"Curiouser and curiouser," I muttered.

That Ghoul Ava Finds an *Appetite for Deception*

Hot for Teacher

When the security voice announced the arrival of four humans, I was at first confused. Then annoyed. If that idiot thought he could save his skinny white butt from the block by bringing along his friends, all he had really done was place them in jeopardy as well.

I had Rock open the door, and was impressed by how unperturbed she appeared. Didn't she realize that we were probably going to have to kill at least one of these guys? I didn't want to, and that would not stop me from trying to save Axl, but that bass player simply knew too much. And I bet that is the first time that line has ever been used about a bass player. Go ahead, ask some of your musician friends…I bet they'll laugh themselves silly.

I had to stay back at the end of the entry hall to avoid any sort of contact with the sun and chose to take up a pose of leaning against the bannister of the stairs in as casual a stance as I could manage while being almost angry enough to chew nails and spit thumbtacks. How could this guy be so insensitive and callous to his bandmates and possibly even friends? Not that every band is just one big happy family, but still.

"Holy crap," Izzy gasped as he walked past Rock and entered my house.

Right on his heels was Sorum. The slight-but-athletic

drummer sauntered in like he didn't have a care in the world. And why should he? He had no idea that his life was in danger. Next to enter was BC Slash. His black wig gone, he had long, blond hair pulled back in a ponytail. Like he needed to be any more delicious? Blond haired, blue eyed guitarist? Yes, please, Ava likey very much. The angel (or whatever it was on the other shoulder) slammed images of Race into my head and I had to fight back a nasty frown as my eyes drank in the gorgeous guitarist.

Bringing up the rear was Duff. He stopped in the doorway and looked back and forth between me and Rock. I could smell the fear coming off him in waves and that made me smile. I pulled my sunglasses down. I'd slipped them on as soon as I'd been warned of their arrival. I made eye contact with him once I knew that the other three were looking elsewhere. I gave him a nasty wink that I hoped conveyed all the menace I felt directed at the man at the moment.

"Gentlemen," I said, pushing away from where I was leaning as Rock shut the door, "let me introduce my friend, Rock."

"Like Cher...or Madonna?" BC Slash asked, scratching his head in confusion.

Wow, so pretty, but I had to wonder what danced around in that head. That thought was quickly replaced with a sound scolding by what apparently had to be my conscience. Me, of all people, passing judgement on another person's intellect.

"Sure," Rock said.

My head whipped around so fast I felt my neck pop. I looked at Rock and had to force my mouth shut. She was blushing like a schoolgirl who'd just had her first period right in the middle of gym class while wearing white shorts. (Did all you boys just cringe when I mentioned the "P" word? Seriously, if you think it is a problem for you, try being the recipient. That was one thing I didn't miss now that I was a ghoul.)

"Is that short for something like Roxanne or Rochelle?" Sorum asked. He'd walked up to the Templar. The top of his head barely came to her ample breasts. She also was packing on enough muscle that I would guess she weighed twice as much as he did. That the grown man looked like a child standing beside her is perhaps the best comparison I can give you.

"Rock Star Hell," the woman said coolly.

"Were you born on a commune?" BC Slash gasped.

I saw my friend shoot me a look that clearly demanded that I extricate her from this situation. Oh, and yes, I did just use the word extricate in a sentence. Thank you very much *Word-of-the-Day* calendar.

"Rock is a roller derby queen," I piped up.

"Seriously?" Izzy appraised the Templar with raised eyebrows.

I glanced over and did yet another double-take. He'd walked in with empty hands, yet somehow, he had produced what looked like a pizza folded in half and was taking a big bite from it.

"Yeah," Rock said. "Why, you got a problem with that?"

"Umm...no," Izzy replied. "I just don't think I've ever met a roller derby jock before. Personally, I think it's kinda cool."

"Yes, well we can all talk about roller derby and other things later," I interjected. "Right now, Rock and I need to speak with Duff in private. How about you guys pop into the living room and play with the entertainment system."

The words were barely out of my mouth when Sorum and Izzy took off like they'd been shot in their tight little buns. BC Slash looked around for a moment and then shrugged his shoulders and followed.

As soon as he was out of the room, I spun on Duff. "What the hell are you trying to do, get them all killed?"

The man took a step back which only put him closer to Rock, who was still watching through the archway that led to my living room. Apparently I wasn't the only one who'd noticed their buns.

"I just thought..." he tried to explain, but the words died on his tongue.

"You thought that there was safety in numbers," I snapped. "What you have effectively done is condemn them to whatever decision is made tonight regarding you and what you know."

"You'd kill all four of us?" he gulped.

"I would've preferred to keep it to just you," I shot back.

"So you were totally serious?" Duff already had a pale complexion, but he was now so white that a glass of milk would look dark and dirty next to him.

"You have no idea what you have stepped in," I said. I shot a look over at Rock. She was still mooning. "Hey, Eileen, a little help here?"

The woman shook her head and then gave me a nasty glare. I just shrugged and then nodded to Duff. To her credit, she composed herself quickly and then glanced down one of the hallways that led off from the main entry hall.

"Do you have a room that we can go to and speak privately?" she asked.

"Sure," I answered as I walked past her and led the way to one of the who-knows-how-many rooms that my keep has. I opened the door and ushered the two in ahead of me. I took a step and found myself bouncing off of Rock's chest.

"Sorry, Ava, but I need to speak with Duff alone." I opened my mouth to protest, but she held up one meaty finger to silence me. It had her Templar ring and she tapped it for emphasis. "This is actually pretty serious stuff, Ava. As the acting senior Templar, I have to deal with Mr. McLuvin personally."

I stepped back and gave the nervous looking man a shrug. "Sucks to be you," I said, and then pulled the door shut behind me.

I could've listened in if I'd wanted to, but I ordered my security system to secure the room so that nothing could be heard. Since I had no idea how long that was going to take, I didn't see any harm in checking in on my other three guests.

The massive screen was showing a classic *Guns-N-Roses* concert and the three men were watching with more than just an entertained eye. It was strange, but each of them seemed to be committing it to memory. Izzy was standing off to one side, slouching, his head dipped low and an imaginary guitar in his hand as he basically affected the personality of his namesake. BC Slash was slinking over on the other side of the room when all of a sudden he took off at a sprint just as the person he portrayed did the same thing.

"Excuse me," I finally said when it was clear that none of them had noticed me enter the room.

I guess I expected them to be embarrassed or something. After all, here these men were, aping the movements of one of what has to arguably be considered one of the greatest rock bands of all time in my living room.

"Hey, Ava," Sorum said with an easy smile from where he sat perched on the back of my sofa like he was on a drum riser.

"So…what's with…" I waved my arms, "…all this?"

"Just taking the free time to get down some of the stuff for the new set we are building," the drummer replied, grabbing my encyclopedia-sized universal remote and pausing the picture. Seriously, there must be something in men's DNA that makes them just understand how a remote works no matter how many buttons it has.

"Ummm…okay?" I didn't understand what he could possibly mean.

"Axl is a stickler for the details," Izzy spoke up. "He picks a specific show by the band and then our job is to re-create it."

"Why?" That seemed like a logical question.

"When people come to see a Tribute Band, our job is to maybe give them back a piece of their younger days. Hell, some of them may have never had the chance to see the real band perform and we will be the closest thing they will ever get. While we would never dare to claim that we are as good as the real thing, we make sure that we are the best Tribute version to hit the stage. We've been doing this for over a decade and a half now, and we do our best to give the people the most authentic experience they could ever imagine next to seeing the real thing."

"But you're still just a cover band, right?" I saw all three faces stiffen. Apparently I'd said something wrong.

"A cover band plays a selection of popular songs," Sorum

said coolly. "Usually they focus on an era, but not even that is for sure. A Tribute Band spends all their time honing their skills to bring the audience the music of one artist. There is a *big difference* between the two."

I guess I would take his word for it. Of course, now that I thought back to the show, I'd been pretty blown away by how much they looked and sounded like the real thing all the way down to that little shimmy-slither that the real Axl did when he sang.

"So there are other Tribute Bands like you?" I asked.

"There aren't any like us," BC Slash scoffed, sounding like the rich prom queen talking to the poor girl in the knock-off version of the same dress.

"What BC is trying to say," Sorum hopped off the couch, shooting the guitarist a look, "is that we consider ourselves the best *Guns-N-Roses* Tribute Band there is. We work hard at the details and believe that is what sets us apart from the others. But to answer the question I think you were asking, yes there are other Tribute Bands. Lots of them actually."

"Poison?" I dared to ask.

The three looked at each other and smiled. "Yeah, there's a Poison Tribute Band," Izzy finally said. "They're called Poison'us, I think."

I felt warmth flood to all my mommy parts. If those guys put even half the energy into adopting the look of their namesakes that these guys did…I might just have a new hobby to take up my spare time. I mean, these guys were rock stars, right? They probably had a few groupies.

"You should come to our big outdoor music festival this summer," Sorum continued. "There are like seventeen or eighteen Tribute Bands over two days. You would get a taste of just about everything."

"Yeah," BC chimed in. "It's called Harefest and it is seriously kickass!"

It sounded like fun. Maybe I would try to catch some of it. Of course, it would be a total bummer that I would miss a good portion of it since it was held during the summer and I had to guess that bands started playing during daylight hours.

"So, where's Duff?" Sorum asked.

"He and Rock are discussing some stuff about the abduction of Axl," I answered, feeling good that I wasn't really lying.

"Since you've asked us a few questions, maybe I could ask you a couple?" Izzy said as he licked the last of the crumbs or whatever from his fingers.

"Go for it," I said with a wave of my hand. As soon as the answer left my lips, I wished I could get it back. I had a feeling I already knew what the first question would be.

"Do you two have some sort of skin problem?" Izzy nodded at me and then over at Colt. "It's not contagious or something, is it?"

I'd all but forgotten that the male ghoul was even present. He'd just been silent, tagging along or maybe he had left and come back. I honestly couldn't say. I started scouring my brain for an answer that was at least somewhat plausible. Unfortunately, I was already so twisted up because I'd just realized that I'd been absolutely and pretty much unforgivably careless, that nothing was making itself clear in my brain.

"It's a genetic condition, so no, it's not contagious," Colt spoke up.

I did a quick double-take his direction and felt my belly flutter when he shot me a wink and a smile. In all the conflict, I'd forgotten how All-American-Boy-Next-Door handsome he was. In fact, I was in a room full of men that would make any red-blooded woman just a bit flushed.

"Are you two related?" BC asked, cocking his head like a puppy that heard a dog whistle for the first time. "I would've never guessed it. You don't look anything alike." He paused for a second as his nose wrinkled and his eyes squinted in what I was guessing had to be his brain trying to ferret out the situation and what to say next. "Except for the gray skin, that is."

"Distant cousins," I chirped, mentally patting myself on the back for coming up with what I thought to be a pretty good reply.

"Sweet," BC sighed, "so you guys aren't like, dating or something."

"Umm...no," I coughed.

"Here we go," Izzy groaned, and sauntered towards my kitchen with Sorum right on his heels.

Glad to know they felt so comfortable in my house. Part of me wished that they could see the cluster of goblins following them around. That might give them pause.

"Maybe we could go out for coffee or something?" BC said, easing down onto my couch, patting the spot beside him.

There was a part of me...actually, one part in particular, that would've loved to be able to just accept his invitation. Unfortunately, BC was a human. There was no way in hell we would ever—or *could* ever—hook up.

"She has a pretty serious boyfriend," Colt said.

This time, the look I shot him was much closer to a glare. It was a waste of a really good frown since Colt was now headed into the kitchen where Sorum and Izzy appeared to be trying to figure out a way to turn a majority of the contents of my fridge into a sandwich. This was not the sort of help I needed. The way I saw it, BC would've been good for some casual flirting over the next few hours—provided Rock didn't tell me that we would have to kill Duff and his friends.

"Oh, bummer." BC Slash pursed his lips, and then his expression brightened. "Do you know if your friend Rock is seeing anybody"

And that moment, the of feeling special washed away in an instant. Fortunately, I didn't have to answer the question. Just then, I heard the door to the room that Rock and Duff had gone into open up.

I would've held my breath if it was necessary. As it was, I felt my stomach tighten and start to churn. Things could very suddenly take a turn for the worst and I steeled myself for that possibility.

Fortunately, I only had to do so for about three seconds when the sounds of laughter drifted to my ears. I seriously doubted that either of them would be laughing if Duff was about to be killed.

When the two strolled into the living room, my eyes instantly spotted the change. Duff was wearing a plain metal band like the one I'd seen on Lisa's hand when she'd first been taken in as a Templar-in-training (or whatever they call them). Rock shot me a very slight nod and curved her lips in a smile.

Of course, my brain was already going back to BC Slash's last question about her availability. Not to sound like too much of a bitch, but she was not the sort of women that I imagined men like BC Slash asking out on a date. For one, she was practically twice his size. Also, he was sporting that "pretty boy" look with his long, blond hair and blue eyes. Rock was…well, she was exactly what you would picture a Templar warrior/roller derby enforcer woman to look like.

It would be like me dating Nose Wart.

Okay…maybe that is going a bit far, but you have to understand what I'm saying here. This was going well beyond Paula Abdul's assurances that *Opposites Attract*.

"Guys?" Duff called. "You can head back, I'm gonna be here for a bit talking business with Rock and Ava. No need for you guys to have to endure the boredom."

As he was speaking, Izzy and Sorum both strolled back into the living room. Each of them held a sandwich that would impress a professional *Jenga* player.

"Like, we just made this sandwich, man," Izzy complained.

"You can take it with you," Duff said with an edge to his tone that I found a bit harsh.

As this scene was playing out, another one was unfolding right behind me. Not for the first time in my life, I cursed my exceptional hearing as I had to endure BC Slash's onslaught of come-on lines to Rock. I wasn't sure which was worse, some of the drivel oozing from his mouth…or the girlish giggles that were escaping the lips of the massive Templar warrior and roller derby terror.

"C'mon, BC, I don't need an anvil to fall on my head to know when we ain't wanted," Izzy stage-whispered as he sauntered to the door.

"Thanks for a lovely dinner," Sorum said around a mouthful of sandwich as he stopped in front of me, wiped his hand off, and extended it to me in a handshake. I shook his hand and noticed that he didn't flinch at the coolness of my skin.

I watched the trio leave. I spun to Duff, prepared to ask him what had been said and froze when a long, wistful sigh distracted me. Rock was still staring at the closed front door with an expression that had everything but animated hearts thrumming where her irises should be as well as little cartoon cupids circling her head firing their little love darts at her.

"Hey!" I walked over to Rock and snapped my fingers in front of her eyes. "Snap out of it."

Seriously, if I didn't know better, I'd swear that she was bewitched or something. She was acting like a lovesick puppy, for crying out loud.

"Huh?" She turned her head down to me and just gaped at me with a goofy expression on her face for a handful of seconds until the rational part of her brain kicked in and shoved all that other nonsense away. I mean, BC Slash was certainly dreamy, but this was a touch on the ridiculous side.

"Are you okay?" This time I clapped my hands in hopes that she would shake off whatever the heck was turning her into this ridiculous creature.

"She is fine," Duff said.

There was something in his voice that set me on the defensive right away. I spun, my switch digits already extending.

"Talk fast or I'll gut you here and now," I snarled.

"Exactly the response that I hoped for," Duff said with a slight incline of his head. He uttered something in a language that I didn't recognize and Rock went stiff, her eyes glazed over and her goofy expression replaced by absolute blankness.

I lunged, aiming myself at the midsection of whatever the hell was standing in my living room. Just before I would've made impact, he seemed to melt before my eyes. I landed and spun to see him rematerialize right where he'd just been standing. Once more he was facing me, and his smile hadn't changed a fraction.

"Security?" I called out.

"Yes, Ava?" the voice purred.

"I need you to contain the intruder." I flashed a nasty smile at Duff. I didn't know who or what he was, but I knew what my elven-installed home security system could do.

"Please specify," Sexy Security Voice said.

"The man standing just a few feet in front of me."

There was a pause. The expression on Duff's face had not changed one tiny bit.

"I am sorry, Ava, I detect no man in your vicinity."

Uh-oh.

"Okay," I drew that word out until it almost became a question. "Then what do you detect standing directly in front of me about six feet away?"

There was another pause. If it was possible, a bead of sweat would've rolled down my temple and my lungs would've burned from me holding my breath as I waited for the answer.

"Scan incomplete," Sexy Security Voice answered.

I considered my options. I could go a few ways with this, but they all ended the same. I decided that it was best to skip all the nonsense and just do what I needed to do.

I launched myself at whatever Duff was once more. The results were the same. He melted into the floor and reappeared by the time I spun around to face him again.

"Ava, perhaps I can save you some trouble," Duff said. "I am Godfrey McLemore." He said that like it was important. I suppose that it was to him. To me, it was just sounded snotty and snobbish.

"Yeah? So," I shot back, once again wishing that I had a staff of witty writers coming up with clever quips I could sling back at the multitude of villains that I seemed to encounter.

"You have not heard of me." He'd more mumbled that last bit than say it out loud. He almost sounded upset in a sad way about it. He somehow managed to find a way to stand even straighter which gave the appearance that he was a couple of inches taller. "Are you absolutely certain that the name means nothing to you?"

"Are you so sure that it should?"

He opened his mouth and then shut it again. "Perhaps not. Still, I guess I had hoped."

I cast a quick glance over at Rock who remained in what looked like a trance. It also dawned on me that none of my fellow Supernaturals that called this keep their home were anywhere to be found. I couldn't recall a time that not even one goblin might be sniffing around upstairs for whatever reasons goblins have to do such things.

"How about you tell me and end the suspense," I snapped. My eyes were trying to commit everything about this whatever-it-was to memory. The funny thing was that, the more I tried, the more he seemed to just become a blank slate. There was nothing distinguishable about him...or it.

"I am the Supreme Psychic."

I'd heard the phrase "knock me over with a feather" before, but never really understood it. At least that was the case until now.

Hells Bells

"You mean, like Morgan's boss? That type of Supreme Psychic?" I finally managed to force words out of my mouth. "Then what is the deal with all the games? You intentionally brought humans to my home, you acted like…well…like a human."

"I thought that it might give me a chance to get a better lay of the land versus coming alone." Godfrey McLemore strolled over to my couch and made himself comfortable.

"I'm not buying it," I finally said as I tried to get a reaction out of him by extending and retracting my switch digits a few times.

"I don't care," Godfrey shot back with a cold stare and a non-committal shrug of the shoulders. "I did not come here seeking your approval, simply your compliance."

"Huh, you haven't been paying attention to the reports then." I shot a look over to the door that led to the lower levels of my keep. Where in the hell were my goblins? My bugbears? Anything? I focused on Nose Wart and summoned him, but it felt like my words merely echoed down a long, empty corridor. Something told me that my call would go unanswered. "I'm not real big on the whole complying thing."

He appeared to ponder that statement for a moment. "And that is one of the reasons that I brought those humans with me. I had a concern that you might just kill me out of hand despite the fact that I demonstrated some degree of Supernatural energy when you discovered that I could see your goblins."

"Them's the rules, buddy." I gave him my own indifferent shrug.

"You do not get to make those decisions," Godfrey almost shouted. "That is for the regional Psychic to decide, not you. You are a soldier, a weapon that can be wielded by a Psychic, but you are not the one to make decisions as to who will live or die."

"Right now, Morgan is out of town and left me in charge." Okay, that last part might not be entirely true, but Mister Fancy-pants didn't need to know that.

"That does not give you the right to make a judgement on a mortal. Your sole responsibility in the absence of your Psychic is to maintain the peace and monitor the area for any possible intrusion."

That brought up another point. "So how come I didn't know that you were here? I didn't get any indication that we had a visitor."

"I live here, you simpleton."

"That was uncalled for," I sulked. Suddenly I felt like I'd been sent to the principal's office.

"And your cover is to be the bass player for a Tribute Band?" I scoffed.

"I have lived through some of the most amazing moments in musical history. I was fortunate enough to play twice with Wolfgang Amadeus Mozart as the conductor. I sat in a basement with a young Jimi Hendrix and did session work for The King of Rock *and* the King of Pop."

"What does that have to do with anything?" Okay, I was admittedly impressed, but I wasn't about to let him know that.

"You wouldn't understand." Suddenly this Psychic was the one sounding dejected and a bit thrown off.

"Try me."

"I was in LA when the actual band came together." A faraway look washed over Godfrey's face. I saw what seemed to be a mixture of regret and longing in his eyes. "I had the chance to be their bass player, but I chose a different band thinking that these dysfunctional ne'er-do-wells would implode long before they ever got started."

I thought that over for a second. Was he saying what I thought he was saying? "You had a chance to be in—"

"That is not important!" he snapped suddenly, coming to his feet so fast that I immediately crouched into a defensive posture in preparations for an attack. None came. "I am not here to discuss my personal life with the likes of you."

"Excuse me?" Now I was pissed. "The likes of *me*? Let me tell you something Super Psychic, I don't actually know why you are here. Nor do I care. But you are in my house and you will not talk to me that way or I will gut you like a fish. You got me, Godfrey?"

His pale face turned a deep crimson. Something told me that it had probably been a while since anybody had used that tone with him, much less threatened to gut him.

Ava! a voice barked in my head. *Do you have any idea who you are talking to?*

Yeah, Godfrey McLemore, I answered. *And what are you doing out again?*

But— Mystify tried to protest. I quickly shut him away and hurriedly tied off the confinement. One thing was certain, when things settled down, I was going to find out what I was doing that allowed him to keep escaping confinement.

"You will not address me in that manner or that tone again, ghoul. Do you understand?"

I took a step towards Godfrey McLemore and dropped my voice to its most menacing tone. "If you ever insult me in my house again, those will be your last words."

I wasn't afraid of this guy. Unless he was packing some sort of serious firepower or magic ability, he was in the wrong place to be making demands, much less threats.

He was about to retort, and I am willing to bet that it would've been something that pushed me over the edge. Fortunately (for him), a moan snapped my attention over to Rock. She was blinking her eyes rapidly. I also noticed that her ring had taken on a soft glow. That was new.

"Ava!" Rock finally gasped. Then she blinked her eyes again and looked around with an expression that made it clear that she didn't know how she'd gotten to my living room.

"Welcome back," I said, edging towards her while not taking my eyes off of Godfrey.

"We have a problem..." And then she obviously saw the Psychic standing just a few feet away. "You!"

In a flash, Rock was on the man, her hands going around his throat. He let out a squeak before the air was cut off and began to swat at the powerful forearms belonging to the female Templar.

"I need you to do me a favor, Ava," Rock hissed through clenched teeth.

I noticed that the cords of muscle that made up her arms were bulging and straining way more than they should be considering the obvious size difference. Also, her ring was glowing even brighter now as she fought to keep her hands around the throat of Godfrey McLemore.

"Sure," I said, stepping up beside her.

"I need you to get some salt and one of those squirt guns you keep full of holy water."

"How did you know about that?" I gasped.

"I read your books, but now is not the time, Ava. Go." She grunted with the exertion of maintaining her grip. "Now!"

I ran into my kitchen and grabbed a box of salt from the cupboard. The squirt gun was going to be another matter. The closest one was in one of the armories. I had several located throughout my keep. But the closest one was two levels down.

I dashed back with the salt and was stunned to see that Rock had been pushed back up against the far wall of my living room. Her face was soaked, and rivulets of sweat ran down from her temples. Her hair was sticking to her forehead and I even saw a strand plastered to her left cheek. Also, for some strange reason, Godfrey McLemore continued to struggle. I figured he should be unconscious by now.

"The Super Soaker is downstairs," I said as I ran up, holding the box of salt in my hands.

"Fine," Rock grunted, "you can go get it in a moment. First, I need you to make a circle with the salt around me and…this."

That seemed like an odd request, but I figured that she knew what she was doing. I started pouring salt on my floor and had to turn sideways to get between the wall and Rock at one point.

"Be outside of that circle when you connect the ends," Rock cautioned.

Once more I was puzzled by her request. This was too strange, but I did as she instructed, making sure that I was outside the inch or so wide circle of salt. Okay, it was not a pretty circle, but at least it was round. Ish.

As soon as I was clear and the ends connected, Rock uttered a word in a very ugly sounding language. It was like one of those science fiction movies where the starships have those force fields that glimmer. Rock dropped her arms, but a blade made from some kind of black metal was in her hands in a flash.

"Do you still want that holy water?" I had started for the door to the lower levels, but I'd paused, mesmerized by what I was seeing.

"Yes," Rock said flatly, brandishing the knife in Duffing-ton's face. "I've got things under control now."

I had a million questions, but I was willing to bet they wouldn't be welcomed very enthusiastically at the moment. I hurried to my arsenal and grabbed the Super Soaker that sat on a rack with a collection of high-powered rifles. The room was a weapon freak's wet dream. I didn't know what most of the stuff was called, or what it did, but Race had seen to the stocking of my arsenals personally.

I rushed back upstairs and slammed the door behind me when I realized that, once again, I'd seen no signs of activity below. It was as if my entire keep had been emptied out.

"I got it," I called as I hurried up to where Rock still stood inside the shimmering wall of what looked, sounded, and smelled like electrical energy.

"Fine, now keep it pointed on our little friend here."

"You will pay for this, Templar bitch," Godfrey snarled. Only, it no longer sounded like the man I'd first met as Duff. This sounded like the giddyup-ah-oom-papa-mow-mow guy from the Oak Ridge Boys. His voice had dropped a few octaves, and it had a strange echo to it.

"Not likely," Rock scoffed.

"Umm, can I be let in on the secret?" I asked tentatively.

"We have ourselves a demon," Rock said like it was no big deal.

"Run that by me again?"

"This is the creature that will lead the Supernaturals into society?" Godfrey laughed in his deep, throaty voice that was not in any way appealing or attractive.

"You'll never find out," Rock shot back. "Now, I am going to give you exactly five seconds to vacate that mortal's body, or I will carve you out of there and stuff you into a bottle."

"You wouldn't dare." The thing speaking through Duff's mouth didn't sound convinced of his own words. "Killing a mortal is messy business. It isn't like the old days when murder was so easy to get away with."

"You're stalling and I'm counting."

Rock brought her blade up to the throat of what I now had to guess was a possessed Duff. Only, I'd been told that possession wasn't really an accurate description. It was more like an infection.

"Wait!" the deep voice rumbled. "Let me speak to the ghoul for just a moment, and then I will depart."

Oddly enough, Rock looked like she had to really think about it for a moment. At last, she gave a slight nod of the head.

When Godfrey or Duff, or whatever this thing was, turned to me, I saw something flicker in his eyes. In the literal blink of an eye, I was staring at two silvery orbs.

"You're in over your head, Miss Avangelina Katherine Birch."

As soon as I heard my full name, I knew who I was speaking with. Very recently, I'd encountered a demon by the name of Vinwoanoch. He'd been part of the scheme that ended with Colt's death and subsequent reawakening as a male ghoul. I could bore you with details, but it would be much easier to just read my last little adventure.

One of the things that I'd come away with during that last little exchange was my newest resident, an ogre magi named Keyoggia. Of course I'd locked him away and had help securing him much like Mystify had once been kept isolated. That had been one of the last things that Betty and Blodwen had helped with before things inside my head had gotten all messed up.

"Back so soon, Vinwoanoch?" I said sweetly, although my mood was anything but when it came to this evil creature.

"You know this thing's *real* name?" Rock gasped. "How did that happen?" I opened my mouth and the Templar held up one of her massive hands and began to shake her head vigorously. "Never mind. I don't want to know. Just tell me that you haven't made some sort of offer to this thing."

"Actually, I have an offer for you, Avangelina Katherine Birch." The man's head gave a slight bow, but I saw the hint of a smile curve his lips in a way that was nothing short of sinister-looking.

"Is that so?" I folded my arms across my body and made no attempt to hide the doubt that I felt when it came to anything this demon had to offer.

"If you hand over the ghoul known as Colt Walter Faber, I will see to it that the succubus hands over the human that she abducted."

I hadn't expected that. It would certainly make things easier for me. I hadn't done well in my first meeting with the she-demon. I still hadn't even found out an effective way that I could do battle with her. Demons did not seem to have the same weaknesses as Supernaturals.

"Ava," Rock hissed, her tone oozing with warning.

You can't do this, Ava, a voice said from somewhere deep in my mind. It was so faint that I couldn't tell if it was Betty, Blodwen, or just my own conscience.

"Excuse me, but I'm standing right here," Colt barked.

"Give him to me, and I will remove what will become nothing more than a nuisance for you if you choose to let him continue to stay here." Duff leered at Colt and I saw the normally self-assured man stagger back a step.

"Why go through all the theatrics?" I challenged. Colt started to say something else, but I held up a hand to silence him. "And how long have you been floating around inside of poor Duff here?"

"Avangelina Katherine Birch, you always make me laugh." As if to demonstrate, Demon Duff threw his head back and laughed, loud and deep. "You cannot ask questions of a demon without offering up something of value."

"Right now, the value I am offering is the extra time you have been allowed to remain on this plane or whatever you consider someplace that is not part of Hell, the Abyss, or Detroit." Okay, probably not fair to include Detroit in that list, but have you been there?

Demon Duff seemed to consider my words for a moment. When he locked eyes with me again, I saw something in his gaze that I didn't really like. It was almost as if I'd made the demon angry. Granted, making others angry is sorta my thing, but when it comes to demons, I'd rather be anonymous.

"Perhaps I must rethink my assessment of you Angelina Katherine Birch."

"And perhaps we need to just banish you and be done with this nonsense," Rock snarled. She pressed her blade against its throat.

"Umm, is that gonna kill Duff as well?" I asked.

Rock's shoulders slumped. "Ava, sometimes you have to sacrifice a pawn to take out a queen."

"That is quite generous of you to give me such an assessment Eileen Louise Jakovich," the deep voice almost slithered out from between Duff's lips.

"Let's see how generous you think I am when I send you back through this blade." The Templar's expression almost matched the demon's in its nastiness. "This blade has been blessed by four holy men of different faiths."

I saw the demon try to shrink away from the weapon. The field of energy crackled the instant that he made contact with it and there was a green flash. The stink of sulfur wafted my way as tendrils of smoke curled up from where the Demon Duff had made that slight contact for the briefest of seconds.

"Okay, let's all just calm down," I said, holding up my hands. "First, let me make it very clear that I will not be handing over Colt to you or anybody else." I glanced over at the male ghoul and gave what I hoped was a reassuring smile and nod. Next, I addressed Rock, "And what is the deal with the knife? I mean, obviously there is something special about what you just said."

"A knife like this will bind a demon to its plane for a period of a hundred years." Rock touched it to the throat of the Duff Demon.

"Yes, but if you slit Duff's throat, he dies as well. I'm right about that, aren't I?"

"Ava, I know you still struggle with some of the aspects of your humanity. I did too when I first became a Templar, but it isn't every day that you can send a demon to its plane for an extended period. They are seldom caught. In fact, there hasn't been one banished in that manner in almost forty years."

"And that's all well and good, but you aren't killing Duff," I insisted.

"Ava—" Rock tried to protest.

"This isn't up for debate," I cut her off. "This is my territory, and I have say-so here."

"Actually," Rock let that word draw out for a few seconds, "this is Morgan's territory."

"And she is gone right now, leaving me in charge."

99

"Templars don't fall under any Psychic's jurisdiction."

I could see that this was something the two of us were not going to see eye-to-eye on. The thing was, a part of me knew that Rock was right. We were talking about the life of one person versus condemning a demon to wherever it came from for several decades. I wasn't too savvy on demons yet, but something told me that they could cause a lot of trouble. I'd just dealt with a situation that was engineered by one.

"Okay, demon, listen up," I said. I gestured for Rock to ease up with her blade. It was clear that she didn't want to, but eventually her hand relaxed some of the pressure. "I am going to let you go home. I want you to take the succubus with you. I won't be giving you Colt."

The laugh that came from Duff was as inhuman as any I'd ever heard. "Avangelina Katherine Birch, you are not giving me anything, yet you are asking for my services. That is unacceptable."

"Did you miss the part about not having that knife used on you? I am giving you your life and letting you leave here without being condemned."

"No." The word rang with absolute finality. "You are not making me an offer that compels me to accept it. I know for a fact that you wish this human to be spared. What you perceive as bargaining from a position of strength is actually a point in my favor."

Hmm, I guess I hadn't thought of that. "Okay, how do we sweeten this deal so that you will leave peacefully?"

I could see Demon Duff's face harden with intense thought. The demon mulled over the possibilities for a few seconds. Apparently Rock wasn't inclined to let this bargaining go on for long.

"You have ten seconds, or both of you lose out. I will cut your throat despite Ava's wishes." Rock pressed the blade to Demon Duff's throat again.

"I will depart freely and forfeit my claim on Colt Walter Faber." The demon flashed a smile and started to fold his own arms across his body, but Rock's hand twitched and he thought better of it.

"What about the succubus?" I pressed.

"She is not my concern."

"I need you to take her back with you," I insisted.

"Then offer me one favor."

I opened my mouth to agree. After all, how bad could that be? Apparently pretty bad because Rock cut me off.

"If you even think about saying yes, I will slice this thing's throat right here before the word gets past your lips," Rock warned.

"Then my deal is my final offer. Accept it or your friend here will slit my throat and be done with it." The demon broke from my gaze to look at the Templar. "And do not think for a moment that I will forget this Elaine Louise Jakovich."

I didn't want to test my chances with Rock, and so I nodded my head. "Deal."

As soon as the word was spoken, I heard a chime that resonated throughout my body. There was a flash of light from Duff's eyes, and then the man slumped to the floor. Rock's reflexes were the only thing that kept the blade from doing its job of slitting the man's throat.

"You idiot!" Rock snapped.

That Ghoul Ava Finds an *Appetite for Deception*

10

Foolin'

The Templar stepped over Duff's body, dragging the toe of her boot through the circle of salt. The field of energy made a popping sound like a big balloon, and was gone.

"What?" I asked.

She sounded way too angry for it to be about me wanting to save Duff's life at the expense of a demon not being banished. But then, what did I know?

"You just made a deal with a demon."

Well, that seemed a bit too obvious. There had to be more to her noticeable displeasure than that.

"Did you have a better idea?" I shot back. As soon as she opened her mouth, I finished that statement. "That didn't involve you killing Duff?"

Finally, I got to see what it looked like when a person snapped their mouth shut after the words they were about to say had been taken away. Unfortunately, I didn't have time to gloat.

"Every demon in the spirals of the Abyss will now be very aware that you have a weakness. All they need do is endanger a human and you will give them what they want."

"That's not true," I argued.

"Demons are very cunning, Ava. They will come at you and then offer something outlandish. That will make it easier for them to get whatever it is they really came for."

"You must think that I'm an idiot," I shot back.

I was used to Morgan underestimating me. I was used to most of the big bad beasties that I fought doing the same. It actually made it easier to do my job. I was not ready for somebody that I thought I might be able to call a friend to do it.

"Ava, I don't think that you're an idiot," Rock said, trying to sound consoling. "But I have experience with demons. You have no idea how nasty they are and what sort of damage they can wreak in a relatively brief period."

"But what good would it do for me to make a deal to save Axl if I allow Duff to be murdered?"

"I wouldn't have murdered Duff," Rock maintained. "I would have eliminated a demon. Duff would have been a casualty of that situation. His death would've been an unfortunate consequence, but we would've been free of that particular demon for a long time, and anytime that you can take one of them out of circulation…it is a good thing."

She'd started off fine with her argument, but then she looked away and I saw something in her face just before she did that told me she wasn't being entirely truthful. That was odd. Rock was always one to shoot straight and not mince words.

"You're *lying*." I put a bit of heat on that statement. It upset me that she was not being honest. She was somebody I thought that I could trust.

"Ava, there is more to this than you understand. You are still so grounded in your former humanity. I'm sorry." She made that apology hastily to stop me from interrupting. "It's true, and with what is looming ahead of all of us, the Templars, Psychics, and the Supernatural community, it is not a luxury that you can afford."

I didn't like what she was saying, but at least she was being honest now. I continued to stare at her and wait for her to go ahead and reveal whatever it was that she felt she had to hide or sugarcoat.

"You can't have a war without casualties, Ava."

"Umm, duh." Okay, so not my best retort, but she was still skirting something.

"Until now, the demons have been consigned to staying out of things. They haven't ever been involved in the affairs of Supernaturals, humans, or anything like that aside from the rare abduction. Those were usually because of some foolish deal that a mortal makes with him or her thinking that they are clever enough to outsmart a being that has been forging contracts and then exploiting loopholes for thousands of years. There is a story that says the very first lawyer was actually a demon."

That didn't surprise me. Like the old joke goes: What do you call a bus full of lawyers driving off a cliff? A good start. Yeah, basically lawyers are evil. And if you're a lawyer, please feel free to drop me a line and let me know where I am going wrong on that assessment. Oh…and then I am going to tell all your snobby friends that you read my books and they will probably boot you out of whatever secret club all you lawyers belong to.

"The last thing we need is for demons to become involved in this war. They will sow discord through the ranks and give you yet another front that you will have to fight on."

"I hate to be the one to clue you in, but this all started because a demon abducted a human in my district, so your claim that they stay out of the affairs of humans is pretty much toast."

"Unless this Axl person made a deal with one." Rock leveled her stare on me and folded her muscular arms across her chest.

I hadn't thought of that.

"If he did, I will back off. There has to be a way to find out," I conceded.

"Sure, you could ask the demon. But then you'd have to trust that she wasn't lying to you."

I was about to say something like how amazing I am at being able to tell if somebody is lying to me, but that was the moment Duff chose to stir.

"What the hell?" he moaned looking around the room with a confused look on his face that quickly changed to an expression of fear. "How did I…" His voice faltered and he tried to scoot back, but there wasn't any place for him to really go.

At first I was a bit confused by his reaction. Then I remembered that I'd told him he would be meeting with somebody that was able to judge if he was a possible threat. If he was found to be one, he would die. That thought made me give myself a mental slap in the forehead. Here I was, just moments ago, arguing for this guy's life, but it had been my discovery that he'd grown aware of the Supernaturals—specifically, he could see my goblins, plus, he wasn't buying that my skin color was just some sort of anomaly.

"Just relax, Duff," I said, actually taking a step back in the hopes that he might calm down a shade. At the moment, he looked like he was about to have a heart attack.

"So, you are the human that can see goblins," Rock said, taking a step forward, effectively placing herself between me and the terrified bass player.

"Umm…well…" Duff stammered.

"Ava, could you summon Nose Wart, please?" Rock had her back to me now and it was suddenly as if none of our conversation had taken place. Well, I wasn't put off that easily. We would be revisiting the topic.

I sent out a mental feeler for my little goblin. He arrived a moment later, and the instant he walked in the room, Duff's eyes darted over to him and then back to Rock. If I would've blinked I would've missed it.

Rock waited a few moments and let Duff fidget and start to sweat. Nose Wart walked up to the human and regarded him, cocking his head first one way then the other. Eventually, he came and stood at my side.

"As soon as you see the goblin, let me know," Rock said evenly, her voice displaying almost no emotion.

After a few seconds of silence, I snorted and decided to ask the Templar some questions of my own. "So, I thought that Templars were supposed to be able to detect Supernatural creatures. How did a demon slip past you? Better yet, how did one end up alone with you in a room where you were supposed to be interrogating the human or whatever it is you Templars do."

"You are acting peculiar, Ava," Rock replied. That wasn't an answer to my question and I saw it for a thinly veiled attempt at deflecting and changing the subject.

"Uh-uh," I said, wagging my finger. "I asked you a question first."

"Demons are not something we normally have to be watching for. I wasn't carrying any of the amulets that would indicate one was near. They are normally only worn when needed to minimize the risk that they fall into the wrong hands. The only thing that saved us was my ring. It countered the hex that this demon obviously placed on me the moment we were alone. Coming around in your living room told me all I needed to know at that point" Rock explained.

"Wrong hands?" I went back to the first point she'd made, something about that didn't sit right.

"There is a very specific magic used to create those devices. If the demons were to get their hands on it, they might be able to come up with something that could counter them."

Rock still had her back to me. From the look on Duff's face, she was staring very intently at him. She was obviously waiting for him to acknowledge Nose Wart. The look he had reminded me of somebody that might have an itch or a tickle and is doing their best to ignore it in the hopes that it would just go away. I don't know about you, but it always makes it worse for me.

Here is an example: Imagine that a large, hairy-legged spider somehow managed to lower down from above you and is on the top of your head. It begins to creep down the back of your head until it finds the exposed nape of your neck. Now it is creeping inside the collar of your shirt and trying to make its way down your spine. Have you shrugged violently or even swatted at your neck? If not, did you want to *really* badly? Well, it was obvious that Duff was making it a point to not look at Nose Wart. His eyes were going anywhere the little goblin wasn't.

"Why is he doing that with his eyes?" Nose Wart whispered loudly. The goblin scuttled over to Duff and climbed Rock until he was perched on the Templar's shoulder. "He looks like he's been drinking fermented bugbear piss."

I wasn't aware that was an actual beverage, and a part of me decided to just pretend that the goblin was exaggerating, but something in the way he said it told me that he was serious. Also, the goblin speaking was making Duff's attempt to avoid looking at the goblin that much more difficult.

"Should I poke him?" Nose Wart leaned forward to put himself in Rock's field of vision.

"Do you want to let this continue to drag on? I can assure you that the little goblin will become more creative with ways in which to get you to acknowledge his presence." Rock planted her ham hock-sized fists on her hips and continued to stare down the tall, skinny man.

"I don't want to die!" Duff blurted. "Ava said that my being aware of these things and seeing the succubus and noticing her skin were all reasons to kill me to keep your secret, but I promise, I'll—"

"Yeah, you won't say a word. Do you know how many times I've heard that? And yet, you humans just can't help yourself. Your big mouths have caused poor Vlad to have to vacate his family's castle in Transylvania, families of Sasquatch have had to push deeper and deeper into the forests, and don't get me started on poor Nessie. So, please forgive me if I don't just take your word that you will keep your mouth shut," Rock scoffed.

Each example only caused the man's jaw to drop further. It made me remember back to the first time I encountered an actual vampire. Her name is Belinda, and I can't stand the centuries-old creature trapped in the body of a sixteen or seventeen-year-old girl. But it had been quite a shock when I discovered that vampires and all other sorts of nasty beasties are very real.

"Plea-he-he-hese don't kill me," the man wailed as he dropped to his knees.

"Let me kill it before it embarrasses itself anymore," Nose Wart piped up.

I was almost ready to agree. If for no other reason than to not have to look at the spectacle of a grown man crying like a little baby.

I know that most mortals do not enjoy the thought of dying. And I realize that my being a Supernatural meant that it was possible I could live for hundreds of years, but it was just impossible for me to imagine a scenario where I would cry like a big baby at the prospect of my death.

Sure, easy for me to say…right?

"You don't see anything in this room except for me and Ava?" Rock prodded.

Duff looked back and forth between the two of us and then his head sagged until his chin was resting on his chest. "I see it."

"It?" Nose Wart coughed, scurrying down Rock and planting himself in front of the man. "I am Nose Wart, chieftain of Just Goblins. I am not an *it*, human."

"Okay, we can do this later," I said as I stepped forward and placed my hands on Nose Wart's shoulders. I turned to the Templar with a raised eyebrow. "So, what do we do about this?"

"He has at least some ability to sense things outside of the normal human spectrum. If times were different, I would have him brought to the commander. Unfortunately, we don't have time for that." She had a long and slender blade in her hand before I could do or say anything.

The scene almost felt like everything shifted into slow motion. I know that sounds kinda cheesy and hack-ish, but it's true. All that was missing was a long, drawn out, low-pitched version of my saying, "Noooo!"

As for Duff, his whimpering ended abruptly and his body hit the floor with a meaty thud. Nose Wart glanced down at the liquid spreading out from the body and towards his feet. He looked up at me with a curious expression and then started to laugh. Maybe I could laugh later, but not right at the moment. At the moment, I felt too terrible to laugh. I stared at Duff's body splayed out on my floor; arms and legs akimbo. This was not going anything like I had planned.

11

Wake Me Up Before You Go-Go

"He has urinated in the house, that will not ingratiate him to our hostess," a deep voice rumbled from behind me.

"Theodore," I turned to see the owlbear standing in the doorway to the lower levels with a flock of goblins clustered around his legs, "could you get me the mop and some soapy water, please."

"Yes, Ava," the large creature answered in a voice that was more of a gentle growl. "And then I have been asked to provide a story to the young goblins in the nursery, so if you do not object, I would like to get a book from the library?"

I knew we had one…a library that is. And maybe I should actually go check it out for myself someday, but I just did not have the time to do something as mundane as relaxing and reading. Not that I'd ever considered reading a form of relaxation before, but after a couple of years with my Word-of-the-Day calendars, I don't think I will get as confused as I used to get when I was just plain old Ava.

"Sure." I gave a wave of my hand and turned back to where Duff remained unconscious on my floor.

I knelt and winced when I saw the bruise already starting to darken over his left eye where his face had bounced off the floor when he'd fainted. It also looked as if he'd split his lip.

111

"So," I looked up at Rock who was standing over the unconscious figure with a bemused smile on her face, "what do we do with him?"

"I was planning on taking him on as my own personal plebe, but after this display, I'm not sure."

"He did think we were about to kill him," I reminded the Templar, although that was still pretty lame.

"And how many times have you faced death in just the past six months? A Templar is the shield between darkness and humanity. We face the things of nightmares without fear," Rock stated with an air of pride. "I can't have this pathetic man fainting anytime we get into a nasty situation."

"And were you just ready to take on every furry or fanged beastie that came at you on the first day?" I had no idea why I felt the need to protect Duff, but here I was doing exactly that.

"I sure as hell didn't faint?" Rock snorted, toeing the body on my floor with her boot.

Just then, Theodore arrived with a bunch of young goblins in tow. He had a mop in one paw and a bucket in the other.

"Shall I clean up?" He inclined his head toward the body still sprawled in the pool of urine.

"No, that's okay. I'll take care of it." I took the mop and bucket from the owlbear and watched as he sauntered down the hall, presumably in the direction of the library.

Rock made an exasperated sigh that matched the sour look on her face as she scooped up Duff's limp body and carried him away. A moment later, I heard the sounds of a shower begin. A few seconds later, I heard a yelp. I cleaned up my floor after having to refuse Nose Wart's help twice as he insisted that such tasks were somehow below me.

By the time everything was cleaned up, and I'd put the mop and bucket away, it was actually almost sunset. I could head out soon and try to confront this succubus and get Axl back before she whisked him away to the Abyss.

"Ava?" a voice whispered from behind me and I spun to see Colt standing there with a peculiar expression etched on his face.

"Remember when I told you about that link or whatever that had me thinking there might be a spy here?"

"Yeah?" I replied, curious as to why the man was talking so quietly as he seemed to be scanning the room in search for something.

"It's active. But it isn't up here with us. I think it's someplace below." He paused like he was straining to listen to something. "What was that big creature with fur and feathers named again?"

"You mean Theodore?" I almost laughed as I answered. If he was under the impression that the owlbear was disloyal, I simply would not be able to believe him. It just wasn't in the big guy's nature.

"Yeah..." he said, drawing that word out as he drifted off, once again giving the impression that he was listening to something. "I can hear him reading."

"Okay?" I rolled my hands to indicate that he should to continue with whatever it was he felt he needed to tell me.

"Whoever this is, this traitor, I think it is still here." Colt paused and closed his eyes for a moment and then opened them as he gasped. "And I think they are about to do something horrible."

"What do you mean by horrible?" I pressed, suddenly anxious. I grabbed him by the arm and started towards the doorway to downstairs.

"This whatever-it-is just walked in where that Theodore creature is reading to the little goblins. Its vision is tinted in red and every goblin as well as Theodore are wreathed in black. I think—"

Before he could finish his thought, a terrible explosion rocked my elven keep. An instant later, Sexy Security Voice announced, "There is a fire in the lower levels. Activating fire suppression system now."

"Security?" I called out.

"Yes, Ava?"

"Can you identify the cause of the explosion and the fire?" It seemed like a longshot, but it was worth a try.

"Multiple chemicals enhanced by a twisted curse," the voice reported.

"And can you tell me who or what set off this explosion?"

There was a pause. I waited, curious as to why an answer could be taking so long.

"Non-intruder. Approved resident."

I waited for the security voice to tell me more, but apparently that was as much as I would be getting. Maybe I had to ask a specific question. It had certainly given me a "what" in response to my query.

"Can you identify the culprit?" I asked.

"Non-human. Member of the orc family. Species known as goblin."

"Impossible," Nose Wart snarled. "None of my tribe would dare now that I have quelled the only member that would think to challenge me."

"Incorrect," Sexy Security voice countered.

"Are you saying that there is another that will challenge Nose Wart for leadership?" I didn't think my heart could take that. Sitting on the sidelines while my little goblin friend fought for his life had been very difficult once. I doubted my ability to just watch and wait a second time no matter what goblin code of honor I might be breaking.

"Insufficient information to allow a complete reply," Security said.

Hmm, that was new. So my seemingly sentient home security system did have limitations. I would have to ask Queen Kari about that when I saw her next time.

"Whatever it is, it is downstairs," Colt announced.

He looked like he was about to say something else when he staggered back and clutched at his head. My first reaction was to think that he had been attacked somehow through whatever link he had with this saboteur.

"This whatever it is just threw three of the goblin pups into the flames." Colt opened his eyes and looked at me with a mixture of dread, fear, and horror.

I took off at a run. I had no idea what was going on, but it was happening in my house and that meant it was my job to crush this myself. I heard Rock calling after me, but, big surprise, I ignored her. When I went through the door, I slammed it behind me.

"Security, lock the door behind me and do not let anybody from the upper level come through," I ordered.

"Lockdown initiated," Security chimed.

I followed my nose like Toucan Sam and sought out the source of the smoke and fire. And if you don't know who Toucan Sam is...you have my pity.

I rounded a corner and saw flames licking the walls from a doorway. That seemed like my target destination. I brought on my switch digits and Sharkmouth and then sprinted the rest of the way. When I reached the open doorway, I could smell all sorts of yummy things. That was the good part. The bad part was that it was the result of at least a dozen young goblins that had been burnt to a crisp.

A low bellow came from the room and my eyes darted over to a large figure in the far corner of the chamber that was obviously too big to be a goblin. It was severely burned and flames were still dancing on parts of it.

"Theodore!" I cried, and rushed into the room. I felt the heat from the fire instantly begin to stretch my skin tight as the waves of heat rolled over me.

I jumped over the charring corpses of the goblin children (had Colt called them pups?) and landed beside the smoldering form of the big owlbear. I didn't know what else to do, so I scooped him into my arms so that I could at least carry him out of this room. I could check him over more closely once he was safe...or at least safer. More safe?

Anyway, I reached the corridor in one leap and laid Theodore down on the floor. Most of his feathers had been scorched to the point of non-existence. The fur had fared only moderately better. Maybe because it was thicker or something, I have no idea.

"The...young ones," Theodore croaked, his voice sounding

if perhaps his vocal cords had been burnt to a crisp along with his outside.

"Don't worry about that right now," I shushed. I glanced into the room and saw that none of the little goblins were moving.

Once I was certain that nothing in that room was alive, I looked up and down the hallway. Doors were set at intervals along both sides. Colt had said that somebody (or thing) had actually tossed a couple of the small goblins into the room after the blast and once the fire had grown.

I cursed myself. I'd allowed pretty much any and every Supernatural that asked to be allowed to come live under my roof. I had no idea what sorts of creatures I'd opened my home to. Apparently at least one of them has no qualms about roasting young goblins.

"You must stop her, Ava," Theodore coughed. I had no idea if he'd said something prior to that since I was so in my own head, but he had my full attention now.

"Stop who?" I asked.

"The goblin…she means to kill all the young ones…and their father."

Since several of the goblins had given birth to litters in just the past few weeks, his answer wasn't giving me anything solid to go off of. I would need him to be more specific. And I really wanted the answer, but as much as I did, I needed to get the owlbear some help first.

That was my next problem. I had no idea who or what I could call that might be able to help. It wasn't like I could just take him to a vet; and I certainly couldn't take him to a regular people hospital.

"I need to get you some medical attention," I said, my head twisting and turning as I looked for anything that might provide me with some much-needed help.

"I am afraid there is nobody here that can provide me with that sort of assistance," Theodore wheezed. "Perhaps it would be best of you allow me to go in peace."

"You mean die?" I shook my head. "That ain't gonna happen."

"I do not believe that my injuries will allow me to survive through the night, Ava." Theodore said this with the same passive certainty that somebody might use if asked if they thought that the sun would rise tomorrow.

"Over my dead body," I snarled as I looked around the room of crispy carnage.

"I would prefer it be over the body of she who has perpetrated this act of treachery and cruelty," Theodore wheezed. His beak/maw was cracked and charred, and it looked like even his tongue had been scorched; unless owlbears have black tongues. I guess I hadn't ever bothered to pay attention.

"So who did this?" I asked.

"Sadly, I have not learned many of the names of the goblins here. The males see me as a threat, and the females have no use for me since I am neither good for breeding, nor am I a warrior. My only connection has been with the children during my time that I spent reading to them. And even that has only ever been temporary. As soon as they are a handful of months old, they are no longer interested in my story time."

Until today, I hadn't even been aware that Theodore was reading to the goblin youngsters. I knew he was almost always seen with a book in his feathered paw, but I guess I assumed that he was just reading for his own benefit.

A thought began to bloom in my mind. Part of me wanted to push it away and dismiss it as my own personal issue, but it was like a popcorn husk stuck between your teeth. You know the kind. The ones that you almost have to slice away a section of your gums to get free and by the time you do excise the bit of corn shell, you feel like you just underwent oral surgery without any anesthesia.

I gave one final appraising glance at the owlbear, told him to hang in there, and then I took off up the corridor. I had one place in my keep that I could find without any problems. It was the one place in the lower levels that I visited with any regularity.

"Security, is there anything that can be done for Theodore?"

117

It seemed like a longshot again, but the home system had already shown that it was more than just an inanimate voice.

"Faeries." That single word wasn't much, but it was all I had to go by at the moment.

"Security, send the word to Rain that I require her assistance," I shouted to the empty hallway as I took one turn after another until I saw my destination up ahead.

I stopped at the door. I'd recently watched an old episode of *Big Bang Theory* where they mentioned some theory called Schrödinger's cat. It had something to do with putting a cat in a box with poison and until the box was opened, the cat supposedly existed in two separate realities. In one, it could be dead, in the other...alive. Until the box was opened, it stayed in that state. (Yeah, just trying to explain it no matter how poorly gives me a headache.)

I let my head roll on my shoulders once, and then I grabbed the doorknob. I felt a tingle of electricity course through me.

"Please don't be a dead cat," I whispered.

I threw the door open to the goblin warren that I'd chosen as my destination to find...nothing. The main room was empty and there was no sign of little goblins running around the place. Normally, this room was a hive of activity. Between all the little goblin pups, the wet nurses flopped around the floor with three to five of the pups feeding at any given time (which took some serious getting used to, I'll have you know), and the adolescent males and females wrestling and brawling with one another in a variety of no-holds-barred skirmishes, this room had never been even close to quiet during any of my visits.

I ventured inside and immediately caught the heady aroma of fresh death as soon as I crossed the threshold. One of the things about every room in my keep was that it was initially set to isolate any sounds and smells from being detectable outside the confines of the room. The way it had been explained to me was that, while the Supernaturals living under my roof were supposed to be under a truce the moment they chose to live here, it still did not do any good to wave a juicy steak in front of a starving person and not expect that person to take a bite. I guess some of the creatures living with me were natural enemies in the real world.

I was almost positive what I would find, but I ventured to the first small room that was set off from the main entry area. Three goblin children no older than a few days old looked to have been hurled at the wall with incredible force. There were three individual and very nasty blood splats and smears down the far wall. On the floor in a heap were the mangled little bodies.

This particular warren belonged to Nose Wart and Teat Mucous. Any of the younglings found here would be their offspring. If things weren't bad enough, I was now going to have to tell my little goblin friend that his children were all dead. As I went from one room to the next, I confirmed that the occupants had all died grisly deaths, and there were no survivors present that I could locate.

I stepped out into the hallway and collected myself. This did not make any sense. The only thing it did was solidify my suspicions as to whom the culprit might be. Since all the servants and wet nurses were scattered among the dead, and there was only one body unaccounted for, I was about as sure as I could be as to this maniac's identity.

I sniffed the air, but the hallway was giving me back nothing. My super hearing was equally useless since the rooms were designed to prevent me or anything else from hearing what might be going on beyond the arch of the door unless I activated a change at each one…and that would take forever.

"Security, locate the goblin Teat Mucous, please," I called out, hoping it might help.

"I am sorry, Ava, but goblins are like grains of sand. They can come and go so fast that my system does not catalog them specifically. I only keep tabs on the total number," Sexy Security Voice replied like she was inviting me to mate.

Maybe later, when I wasn't so occupied, I would ask if there was a way to make the voice a bit drabber and monotone. For now, I would just have to put up with what I thought was an almost inappropriately sexy voice. I also decided that, no matter what the outcome of my quest to bring the tone down to something more security-ish, I would now call the voice "Sadie."

"Okay, can you at least tell me where the nearest living goblin is located?" I asked, deciding to try a different tactic to gain the information that I needed.

There was only a brief pause when Sadie replied, "Approximately ten feet behind you...nine...eight..."

I have no idea how she managed to elude my hearing or sense of smell. After all, she was in the hallway. As I spun to face her, I had no doubt that I'd correctly guessed the culprit. Nose Wart's mate, Teat Mucous was charging me with a wicked looking blade in each hand.

I just managed to jump to the side and let her fly past me in a whirl of flashing metal. These were not the typical goblin weapons. For one, there was not a speck of rust on them. Goblins were not big on cleaning their utensils of death. Something about the bloodstains being an honor and demonstration of their prowess in battle. Whatever.

"You really are an idiot," I snarled as the she-goblin spun to face me. She kept her distance now as she studied me, presumably looking for a weakness to exploit. "You had everything here, and you are throwing it all away. Can I at least ask why?"

"You are the bane of all living goblins, ghoul," she spat. Yeah, I mean literally. She said that and then spat on my floor. "You are a filthy corpse not deserving to take up space among the living you walking pile of a demon's anal scrapings."

Oh goody...I forgot how vile goblins can be when they start hurling curses. But I wasn't fully understanding where this mindset of hers came from. It was the sort of thing that I heard from some of the Templars that were seeking my death. I wasn't aware such prejudices existed among goblins.

"And why would your obvious hatred for me lead you to try and have your mate killed?" I was certain now that she had been the driving force behind the wedge that built between Belly Ulcer and Nose Wart. In truth, he had not been the leak. It had been this little bitch the entire time.

"His loyalty is not to me, or even his clan. His loyalty is to *you*. He treats you like you are a goddess worthy of our supplication."

Wow, those were a lot of pretty good reasons. Still, Nose Wart was very involved in his clan. I'd seen him working directly with a lot of the young goblins, teaching them the things I imagined goblins were supposed to know. Basically how to fight, spit curses, and hurl insults. You know…goblin stuff.

"All of this because you are jealous?" I scoffed.

Okay, that was probably not the best response, but seriously, did this confused little creature think that there could or would ever be anything between me and Nose Wart. If the situation wasn't so horrific with all the dead goblin babies and those two scary looking blades that Teat Mucous was holding, I might've actually laughed out loud. I mean seriously laughed…out loud. And not 'LOL', which usually means the person did not, in fact, engage in laughter.

"Jealous?" the she-goblin snorted. "No, nothing about you could make me jealous. You are an abomination. You are not supposed to be. You are without your soul, and that means you should not exist. I am here to correct that by cutting off your head and then carving out your insides and burning them in a fire of purification."

Now I was positive that somebody had been filling this little creature's head with some twisted ideas. I was also convinced that it was a human. To be precise…a Templar. That would be the only reason this goblin would be speaking this way. In my experience with them, goblins were not very high-minded. They ate when hungry, had sex whenever and wherever they felt the urge…basically they operated on a very primitive level. Nose Wart was different from most. His answers were not just grunts and snorts.

I guess the best comparison I could give their frame of mind was perhaps like a ten-year-old. They were very want-based in their actions. They could speak, but not at a very high level, just well enough to make their point in the most basic manner. I knew that there were certain creatures that they did not care for, but this stuff being tossed at me by Nose Wart's mate were not ideas that a goblin would come up with on their own. Even my Nose Wart, as advanced as he seemed for a goblin, would not be able to wrap his mind around an idea like that without help.

"So, who have you been hanging out with?" I asked casually.

"Hanging?" Teat Mucous wrinkled her nose. I saw the confusion in her eyes. She did not speak to humans much, in fact I might've been her first. Slang terms were too much, and that was further reason that I did not think she came up with this seemingly sudden hatred on her own.

I had a thought. What if there was another demon inside of this goblin? Could goblins be possessed or infected or whatever the term is?

"Tell me who you have been seeing that has filled your head with these new thoughts." I had to take a step back as Teat Mucous jabbed at me with the two blades.

I watched her eyes to see if maybe something would reveal itself. The part of me that had never really liked Nose Wart's choice in a new mate didn't want to see anything that might reveal a demon living inside her. Still, there was a part of me that really didn't want to be responsible for the death of another of Nose Wart's wives. Sure, it would only be the second…but that was the problem. I shouldn't be responsible for the death of *anybody's* spouse.

"The Supreme Knight has eyes and ears everywhere, ghoul," Teat Mucous snarled. "His message is spreading…even under your own roof. You believe yourself to be some sort of divine being spoken of in the prophecies of heretics."

Now I was certain that these weren't her words, but they still stung. For one, I didn't consider myself a divine anything. And as for these rumored prophecies, I keep hearing about them, but I have yet to see one.

"So you aren't alone in this?" I asked. "But you are alone now." I gave a nod to the blades she held. "You really think that you can take me? I don't care how many swords you wield, or how big they might be…there is more to a fight than the choice of your weapon."

Great, now I am sounding like a fortune cookie. All this talking wasn't really my style. At least not if I was going to fight somebody. That made me remember back to a lesson Race taught me during one of our sparring sessions. He'd said something to the effect that, if your opponent is doing a lot of talking, they are either stalling until help arrives, or they are scared of you.

"All I need to do is hit you once," the goblin snarled.

She came at me again in a whirl of blades. I danced out of reach again, but now I was actually concerned. What did she mean when she said that she only had to hit me once? Were these some sort of super-weapon made by the Blue Steel forges?

I felt the wall against my back and realized that I'd reached a corner. That almost cost me as the goblin sensed my momentary hesitation. She came in low and I had to vault over her. I did a summersault in the air that would've made any gymnast proud and landed on my feet. I spun quick so that my back wasn't to my enemy and had to throw myself sideways to keep from being sliced with a vicious backhanded swipe.

"Are you certain that this is what you want?" I asked as I put enough space between me and the whirling dervish of death. "It's not too late, and nobody has to know."

A voice in my head that did not belong to any of the current residents told me that I was making the classic action film mistake. For some stupid reason, the heroes often let the bad guys get away. Later, they come back even worse and do more damage that could've been avoided if they would've just killed the bad guy (or girl) right off the bat.

"I always knew that you were a coward." Teat Mucous spat at my feet. A dark yellow wad of phlegm landed with a revolting splat.

"If that is what you think, you haven't been paying attention," I said with a laugh. "I was giving you a chance. I will consider my offer rejected. So, since I am now going to have no choice but to kill you, can you at least tell me why you killed all the goblin babies?"

The smile I got in response almost made me take a step backwards. It was virtually enough to make me re-visit the idea that she was possessed. There was an evil glee in her eyes that I thought only existed in *The Exorcist*.

"They are the spawn of that worthless Nose Wart. They mean nothing to me."

She brought her arms wide and did a fairly impressive twirl of the blades as she took one step closer. I watched her and tried to gauge a moment when I could lunge in and take her down without getting touched. That was a big switch from just charging in and knowing that I could deal with the problem later by eating a corpse or two. Something told me that those blades were going to be able to take me down permanently, and I wasn't sure that it was necessary for her to land an actual killing blow.

She took two more steps forward and I retreated again to remain out of her reach. I waited for what I thought was an appropriate time and made a swipe of my own with my right hand.

There was an explosion of sparks as my switch digits met one of the blades. I felt a searing pain shoot up my arm and could not hold back the shriek of agony. I staggered back and saw that three of my long nails had been sheared off. Dark, oily smoke rose from my cleanly sliced nails and a stench that reminded me of burning tires filled my nostrils.

My mind scrambled for my distraction mode. As I sought to bring the first song that came to mind into my head I was greeted by…silence. The pain was so apparently consuming that I could not go to my Ava Land. This was simultaneously very new and terrifying. One of the things I'd been taught early on was that a ghoul's greatest strength lies in the ability to ignore, and thus resist, pain.

The goblin lunged again and I threw myself backwards once more. My control was terrible and I ended up flat on my back. On instinct, I planted my hands on the floor to get up and screamed once more as pain threatened to overwhelm me and steal my consciousness.

"All I have heard is how amazing you are, and look at how easy it is to defeat you," Teat Mucous sneered.

"I'm not beaten yet, "I said through clenched Sharkmouth teeth.

Of course, that was me doing as much posturing as the goblin. I honestly had no idea how I would make it out of this alive. The pain was such that my vision was blurring and I could not even make it up off the floor. I was going to lie here helpless until she moved in to finish me off. At that moment, I might have one shot at taking a swipe at the goblin, but if it went as poorly as the previous one, then there was not a lot of hope for this little gray ghoul.

"You will die on your back like the coward I always knew you to be."

Teat Mucous stepped towards me and raised both blades high above her head as she prepared to give the killing stroke. I did not see any way that I could attack with my one remaining good hand, much less the bad one. Also, the stench of burning tires was now changing into rotten tires if that makes any sense. I noticed that my one hand missing the switch-claws was smoking, only the smoke was a very ugly green like the puke from *The Exorcist* but with dark purplish-black hints lacing it.

I did the only thing that I could think of considering the situation: I closed my eyes and waited for the death blow. I would not give that little scag the satisfaction of seeing any fear in my eyes.

When the blow didn't come, I forced one eye to open just a slit so I could peek. For some reason, the female goblin was just standing there. She still had a nasty sneer plastered on her face…well…mostly. Her mouth was still twisted, and her nose was wrinkled, but her eyebrows were raised almost like she was surprised.

Then I noticed it. Jutting from the center of her chest was a jagged and rusty looking blade. Dark blood dripped from the tip and my eyes could not help but follow the single drop as it would grow and then lose the battle with gravity. That drop would plummet to the floor and land with a wet splat.

The blade vanished, and for a moment I wondered if I'd imagined it. That was until Teat Mucous fell facedown onto the floor with a crunch as her face slammed and actually bounced off of the solid surface of a floor that I thought might be some sort of granite. Standing directly behind where my would-be assassin had just been was Nose Wart.

"Please accept my apologies, Just Ava," my little goblin chieftain said with a bow. "I should have been at your side when—" His statement died on his lips and his mouth opened in disbelief as his eyes went wide and threatened to bug out of his head.

I followed his gaze and realized that he was staring at my injured hand. His mouth opened and closed a few times, but no sound made its way out except for just a rasping squeak.

It was as if my inner ghoulness realized that I was not about to die. In a wave, a hunger swept through me that only made the pain of my hand seem to amplify. My gut churned and I almost thought I would be sick.

If my problems were not bad enough, now I was about to be slammed with *Fame Rabia*. That is basically Latin for "Ava hungry...must eat now!" The scary thing about the *Fame Rabia* was that I tended to sort of lose control of my senses.

"I need food," I said, but it was in a voice that was only partially me.

I could feel something else happening. Something was trying to break free in my mind and warn me, but I could not focus enough to concentrate and make whatever that thought was come in clearly.

I felt something in my hands and looked down to see the corpse of a goblin in my lap. That should mean something...shouldn't it? I looked up and saw another goblin. This one was backing away from me and saying something, but the pounding in my head was drowning out his words.

The smell hit me and I looked back down at the body in my arms. It smelled amazing. I opened my mouth and popped the entire body in. I heard a moan that sounded like somebody might be having sex right beside me. I looked around but didn't see anybody…except that one male goblin who had backed up several feet by now.

He was saying something again, but I don't think he was directing his words at me. I heard another voice, but as I climbed to my feet and looked around, I didn't see anybody else.

Ava want food!

I took a step towards the little male goblin. He wasn't dead…yet. I could change that soon enough if he stood still. I licked my lips as I advanced.

Yes…kill. Kill and feed.

That voice came through loud and clear, it also seemed close, but I couldn't see any other living being except for that one male goblin who was still backing away from me slowly. He gave me a 'come here' gesture with one finger and I smiled. Was he going to let me eat him? I took a few quick steps toward him and then the little bastard ducked into an open doorway. I felt a howl of frustration escape my throat.

I peeked inside the room that the goblin had vanished into and saw the equivalent to a Fourth of Ghouly cookout. (See what I did there?) There were barbecued goblins everywhere! It was a feast, and I didn't have to share with anybody. I quickly forgot about that one living goblin and dove into feed. So many of them were actually bite-sized. It was incredible. Something tried to nag at me about this goblin buffet, but *Fame Rabia* made it easy to shove aside whatever misgivings I might try to have as I ate.

I was plucking perhaps the fifth or sixth morsel from the floor when this giant of a woman strolled into the room. Again, there was a part of me that was trying to tell me something. There was something about the woman that screamed threat, yet there was another part of me that was convinced she was not going to bother me. As long as she stayed out of the way and let me eat, we wouldn't have any problems.

That is a Templar…a sworn enemy of our kind. We must kill it, a voice in my head urged. I snorted, maybe inwardly, maybe outwardly—who knows…who cares?—and ignored that voice in my head as I continued to eat.

I popped what turned out to be the last of the teensy, bite-sized goblin treats into my mouth and turned my attention to the half a dozen or so regular-sized ones also burnt to a crisp and scattered about the room. Only once did the large woman make a move in my direction. I gave her my best growl and she retreated, so we obviously understood each other just fine.

By the time I'd consumed the third blacked goblin, I'd discovered that each of them had an added bonus of some sort of creamy filling that trickled down my throat with a glorious warmth. I once again had a very small voice in my head trying to tell me what that might be, but I very quickly decided that I didn't care and continued feasting.

As the final dead goblin found its way down my throat, the haze was starting to lift. For some reason, I fought it. Something about all the stuff that small voice had tried to tell me during my feast was nagging at me and now this new part of my brain was waking up. It was discovering what I'd done and it was apparently not happy.

"Oh, my God," I gasped when the veil lifted and I realized where I was and what I'd done. I looked over at Rock who was leaning against the far wall with Nose Wart at her side. The room was a charred mess, but the nursery I'd discovered earlier no longer had dead goblin children and babies scattered about. None of the goblin wet nurses' bodies were anywhere to be found.

"What have I done?" I almost sobbed.

Oh, yeah…I knew darn good and well what I'd done. But haven't you ever done something really stupid (or terrible) and asked yourself the exact same question? The main difference between you and me is that I often do so out loud. Trust me, if there is a way to stick your foot in your mouth that I haven't found, I'd be very surprised.

"You were overcome with the *Fame Rabia*," Rock said softly.

"You fed to heal, Just Ava," Nose Wart added.

Rock was not my problem right now. And it took all my willpower to force my eyes to meet the little goblin's. I was prepared for perhaps, sadness, maybe even anger. What I wasn't ready for was the absolute acceptance he had painted all over his face.

"I'm sorry, Nose Wart," I choked out, still trying very hard not to cry.

He tilted his head to one side in a mix of curiosity and confusion. He continued to regard me with this expression as he absent-mindedly scratched himself and asked, "Why?"

"I'm afraid I've eaten another of your mates." I looked around the room. "Even worse, I apparently ate the little ones and the wet nurses that were here."

I knew for a fact that goblins ate their mates. As for the children, I really didn't have any idea what they did in that instance. Did they eat them? Heck, maybe they planted them in the yard in hopes that a new one might one day sprout forth. I'm often accused of thinking like a human, and my knowledge of the finer aspects of my Supernatural brothers and sisters is poor at best.

"You honored me with consuming them to heal your terrible injuries," Nose Wart gushed as he took a few steps toward me. "And as for that infected sow's anus that I foolishly gifted with my seed, the only reason that I might've consumed her is simply for the act of crapping her someplace where a bugbear might step in it...or perhaps those ridiculous dogs that now roam around the woods out back."

I was going to take that as him being okay with things. His mentioning that I'd eaten to heal caused me to do a quick switch into full ghoul mode. I breathed a sigh of relief when I discovered my nails were all there and ready for rending, attacking, and perhaps running lightly down Race's spine when he eventually returned home to me.

"Where are those swords she had?" I asked, my head popping up suddenly.

Teast Mucous had made a comment that suggested there might be more like her living under my roof. The last thing I wanted to do was try my luck with those swords coming at me again.

"We have them, Just Ava!" a pair of goblins chimed as they came bounding into the room.

"Let me see those," Rock said, taking a step forward.

"Umm, no offense, but I'm gonna say uh-uh." I stepped between her and the goblins.

I reached for the blades and one hand had barely touched the hilt when a searing pain shot up my arm. I staggered back and saw that the injured arm already looked withered. Also, I could barely lift it.

"That's not Blue Steel work," Rock said grimly. "They have been enchanting the business end of weapons for centuries. Not once have they produced something that had a total enchantment. The power and degree of magic it would take for just one, not to mention a second weapon like that, is outside anything even their best and brightest could achieve."

"As much as I'm sure this history lesson is probably helpful, now is an inconvenient time," I said through jaws clenched together tighter than a homophobe's butt cheeks at a gay pride rally.

I felt the hunger coming back. This was a new experience. I hadn't ever been hit by *Fame Rabia* twice in one hour. Unfortunately, I had cleaned out the nearest available food source just a few moments ago.

"How long do we have?" Rock asked. It wasn't a coincidence that she was already edging towards the door. It made me feel good when I saw that she was herding Nose Wart along with her.

"I...don't...know..." The words fell from my lips like pregnant drops of water from a leaky faucet. I felt as if I might be going backwards into a tunnel.

Eat the Templar! Kill her before she kills us! a voice railed from somewhere in my mind.

My only problem was that I couldn't be sure that voice didn't belong to me. There was something familiar about it, but at the moment, I couldn't place it.

"Stay here," Nose Wart practically shouted, and then took off out the door.

"Wait! Don't..." Rock yelled after him, but the plea died on her lips as the sounds of his feet slapping the floor grew distant in a hurry. "Well," she turned back to face me, "this is...fun."

"I'm not down yet," I managed. That was true, but I didn't have any idea how much longer I would have control over myself.

A look crossed Rock's face. I saw her warring with something internally and then finally come to some sort of conclusion.

"The best I can hope for is that the damage is minor enough that it won't take long for you to recover," she finally said, although I am not sure she meant to say that part out loud. She locked eyes with me. "Do you trust me?"

"What is this...*Aladdin*?" I snarked.

"I'm serious, Ava."

"Fine...I guess."

She took a step towards me and suddenly I was on alert. I felt my fingers and toes go switch in an instant. The big Templar halted her advance.

"We still have a couple of hours before that succubus returns to her plane. But, we have no idea if you will be in any shape to do a thing until you feed. If you flip on me right here, I will have no choice but to try and defend myself." Her eyes flicked to my hands where my claws waited with deadly patience for me to put them to use. "Granted, I would try to subdue you, but neither of us can guarantee the way that might play out. And if I hurt you bad enough, you might be in a state of *Fame Rabia* for even longer."

"And you have a point?" I didn't bother hiding my frustration. If I am being honest, I doubted I had the strength at the moment. I was reverting to something base and primitive. Perhaps this was where the legends of the monster versions of the ghoul came from.

"If I knock you out, then I can secure you and keep you that way until I can get you to your food locker. I'll pull out a body or five and see if that helps bring you down."

It was as good of a plan as any. Did I like the idea of being knocked out by Rock? Nope. But I liked the idea of either me killing her or vice-versa even less.

"What if I don't come around in time?" I blurted as she stepped towards me, pulling a knob-knuckled glove onto her right hand.

"I will do all I can."

I considered those words for a moment and decided to push for clarification. "You mean to save Axl from the succubus, right?"

"Of course," she sighed.

"Do I need to have you swear on it?"

A sour look flashed on Rock's face and she leveled her stare at me. "We're friends, Ava. If I tell you I am going to do something, then that is my word. I shouldn't need to perform a blood oath."

I didn't know what a blood oath was (or if she might just be exaggerating for effect), but I suddenly felt bad for even suggesting. I pulled myself as straight as possible and jutted my chin at her to provide the best and easiest target.

"Just do what you can," I said, my voice a little strained from my chin poking out the way I had it. "Try to wake me before you leave. And if Rain gives you any flak, just tell her I will make amends when I finish this job."

"I will." Rock clenched her fist and drew back.

"WAIT!" I shouted, dropping my chin and stepping back. "Can't you at least give me a countdown? Maybe it will feel less assault-and-battery-y."

"That's not even a word," Rock scoffed. "But fine, I will give you a countdown. On three…okay?"

I nodded and stuck my chin back out.

"One…"

The voice in my head began to scream in rage. Something about killing and rending and eating.

"Two…"

There was an explosion of light, and then the world went black.

That Ghoul Ava Finds an *Appetite for Deception*

12

Surrender

I found myself sitting on the floor of my food cellar. I was just swallowing and felt a tingle in one arm. It took me a few seconds to piece things together. Once it all lined up, I looked over to see Rock, Nose Wart, and Colt standing about halfway up the stairs. My eyes fixed on Rock.

"You didn't count to three," I growled. "That number too high for you or something?"

"Didn't want to give you the chance to duck," Rock replied with a shrug.

I looked down and saw a nasty mess on the floor. Good thing we had a drain in one corner and a power washer to take care of the larger messes. This was certainly one of those.

"Likely story." I climbed to my feet. It wasn't lost on me when both Nose Wart and Colt took a step backwards. "So just how bad was I?"

I began to strip off my clothes. I'd also had a shower installed in here. If I only ate a single body, it wasn't too bad, but when *Fame Rabia* hit, I guess I had the table manners of the Tasmanian Devil. And seriously, if you don't know who the Tasmanian Devil is…you have my pity.

"You tore into the first three bodies like a wood chipper," Rock said, coming to the other side of the shower curtain.

I let the warm water run over my body. I guess I should clarify. I tried a few times to take a shower with Race, but my version of very warm was still cold enough to cause the poor guy to suffer from the Costanza shrinkage. I'll give you a second to figure that one out. On the plus side, I've never had to deal with a fogged mirror.

"Three?" I let the water run down my face and then turned to start on my hair. "How many did I eat?"

"Five."

Hmm, that seemed like an awful lot for just a withered arm. That must be some wicked magic. "And who took the blades in my absence?"

"Nose Wart had a few of the bugbears grab them and take them someplace." There was a long pause, and I could tell that Rock had more to say on the subject. "Do you really think I would turn on you?"

"It's not that, but let's say there was some sort of weapon that was really good at killing Templars, would you want me to have it?"

"There is such a weapon…it's called a ghoul."

"And how close are we to dark?" I decided to change the subject.

"About an hour."

I turned off the water and reached out to grab a towel. When I pulled the curtain aside, I noticed that Colt wasn't on the stairs any longer. Nose Wart had moved down to the bottom step and sat there waiting.

"So, you got any idea how we do this?" I asked as I dried off and then wrapped my hair in that Hindu headwrap that we women are so excellent at while grabbing a second towel and wrapping it around my body. It wasn't that I was concerned about being naked in front of Rock or Nose Wart; it was mostly just out of habit.

I was almost dressed when a thought slammed into me with enough force to cause me to literally wobble in the knees. I grabbed the wall for support and spun to face Rock who was eyeing me with concern.

"Umm, you okay?" The Templar took a step back. "Do I need to get you another corpse?"

"Theodore," I gasped.

"He's fine." I saw Rock's features relax. "Rain and some of the faeries arrived a while ago to deliver a few things they said will help you when you confront this demon. They said they could fix him up and took him to their Sidhe. He was sickeningly excited about that."

"Ooo, toys!" I looked around. Now that I knew the big owlbear was okay, I wondered what sorts of goodies they brought me to carry into battle with a succubus.

Nose Wart scurried up the stairs, calling over his shoulder that he would be right back with whatever the faeries brought. It seemed a bit too convenient, and I looked over to see Rock staring at me with a look that told me I wouldn't like what she was about to say.

"Also, while you were sleeping, I received a summons."

I waited. It was clear that she had more to tell me, and that she was not happy about it.

"Race is missing."

That statement punched me right in the stomach. I think it was in that moment that I realized that my feelings for him were more than anything casual. In fact, they were deeper than anything I ever experienced when I was alive; and that includes my marriage. And I'm not just saying that because it ended in failure. I truly believe that I was experiencing my first real and true love. Race had come to know me as I am. He should be my mortal enemy, yet, through all of that, he treated me better than any man in my life. He saw my strengths under all my insecurity. He never teased me about not being the smartest. Heck, he even saw past my room temperature body, gray skin, and solid black eyes. He didn't try to save me or change me. He simply accepted me.

"What else?" I asked once I was sure my voice wouldn't fail me.

"He was taken by the opposing Templar faction. They say that they will hand him over on one condition." Rock suddenly found something interesting about her fingernails and looked away, breaking eye contact.

"Let me guess. They want me." Her silence was my answer. "When and where?" I pressed.

"They haven't said yet." Rock looked up and I saw something in her eyes that made me take a step back.

I had only known her for a brief time, but in that time, I never imagined there to be anything in the world that could scare her. Yet, what I saw in her eyes was fear.

"So I guess I know what I'll be doing tomorrow." I gave a shrug that did not come close to expressing how I felt.

I was already putting all that mounting anger in a box so that I could save it and use it when I met these people. Like the Emperor in *Return of the Jedi*, I could feel a presence in my head urging me to embrace the hate. I wasn't ready to go that far yet. I was starting to discover that my anger allowed Boudicca to press against her barricade a bit harder. I could not risk letting her out. That also meant I would have to deal with her once and for all very soon.

Can I just say that it hardly seems fair that I don't ever get a happy ending? I mean, I haven't even gone toe-to-toe with this succubus yet, and already I had an impending rescue mission to free my boyfriend from the clutches of a group that really only wanted my death and were apparently okay with using him as bait; and then there is Boudicca.

I still could not understand how the Mother of all Evil had managed to take up residence in my head. I wondered if she would tell me before, during, or after we fought. Of course, if it was after, chances are it would be as she was about to kill me and take control of my body.

"Ava!" Rock snapped her fingers in front of my face. I looked at her and saw that annoyance had replaced fear. I would take that. That was something that I could understand. "I have to go. I won't be able to stay around to help you. Don't kill Duff while I am gone. I will come back for him when this is over. Just tell him to keep his mouth shut until he and I can talk."

"Oh, you have to go *now*?" I said as it dawned on me that perhaps her concern was for more than Race.

"Just a hypothetical question." Rock gave me a nod, but I think she already knew what I was going to ask. "If I die while trying to save Axl, will these guys let Race go?"

"I honestly don't know. Something tells me that things are spiraling in a direction that will lead to the fatal fracturing of our Brotherhood no matter the outcome. Lines have been drawn, and they are as much about basic ideology as they are about whether or not you should be allowed to live."

I wasn't sure how to process that bit of information. "These people are going to contact you again and tell you where to bring me, aren't they?"

"That is what I understand."

"And does that mean our situation changes once you leave? Is this a sort of goodbye?"

"You really don't trust anybody, do you?" The annoyance was clear in Rock's voice. I didn't need to see her clenched jaw or that one vein bulge out on her right temple to know that she was angry. "I'm on *your* side, Ava. We will deal with this situation with Race as best we can. But if you need to actually hear me say the words, no I won't be turning you over to anybody."

"I'm sorry," I sighed. "I guess I really do have some issues to work through. Too bad life isn't inclined to give me that time."

"I have to go, but I'll be in touch." Rock lurched forward and embraced me in perhaps the most awkward hug in history. It was instantly clear that she wasn't used to making these sorts of displays.

She headed up the stairs and I finished getting dressed. By the time I was ready, Nose Wart and a dozen goblins arrived. Nose Wart was carrying what looked like a basic and rather nondescript briefcase. He handed it to me and stepped back. The other goblins assembled in a line behind him.

"We will be accompanying you, Just Ava." The goblin made a bow at the waist and then straightened, sweeping his arm out to indicate the contingent standing at as close to attention as goblins can. That meant there was only minor elbowing taking place. Hey, they're goblins. What are you gonna do?

I knelt and opened the case. There were two canisters and a rolled-up scroll with a wax seal. I popped the seal and read the scroll:

Ava,

This will help you at least have a chance at defeating the succubus. Unfortunately, your task is still very likely to fail. *(Thanks, for the vote of confidence, I thought.)* To have any chance of sending the succubus back, you must circle her with the canister of sea salt obtained from the Dead Sea. You must also be inside the circle with her. As soon as the circle is closed, you must speak the words, *luuke panda*. Lew-YOU-ku PAWN-da. *(Nice, she gave me a phonetic version!)* Once you have done that, you must not touch the salt circle or it will dispel. Also, beware the magical field that you will now be inside. It will be very unpleasant if you come into contact with it. You must then open the second canister. It contains silver ash and you must sprinkle it on the demon. This will bind her. Then you must say *wanya rauko*. WAN-ya RA-you-ko. I wish you well, Ava. Please bring my people home. And I apologize for my crass behavior. Perhaps I must take a page from your book and become a bit more human if we are ever going to return to society.

Rain

Why did that seem strangely simple? Make a salt circle, say a couple of words, and then throw some dust and say a couple more. Was I missing something?

Do you believe that she will simply stand still while you do this? Mystify's voice echoed in my mind.

My initial reaction was to lock him away again, but perhaps he had a point. No matter how untrustworthy he might be, he wanted to survive. He'd already made it clear that my death would be his final end, and thus, he had a vested interest in helping me remain alive.

Probably not, I admitted, feeling foolish for not seeing the obvious. It seemed that every time I felt like I might be making some form of mental headway, I would say or do something stupid to remind myself that I was not the brightest candle on the cake.

I wish I could convince you to abandon this venture, Mystify said solemnly. *I fear that you are in beyond your abilities.*

You won't be the first person to underestimate…oh, wait. You already did that once before. See where that got you?

I am not trying to quarrel with you, Ava. I am simply stating that you will do more harm to the world by dying here and now for a single human than any good that might come if you are successful.

And who gets to make that decision? Do you know what sort of potential this guy has? Maybe he has the cure for cancer somewhere in his head.

Yes, and if he can make a catchy song out of it, then I am sure it will catch on, otherwise, he is just one human in the larger scheme of things, Mystify argued vehemently.

Okay, did I think that this Axl character had the cure for cancer? Nope. But I was not the person or ghoul to decide whose life deserved saving and whose didn't if it was even remotely in my power.

I quickly stuffed Mystify away again and tied off the spell to at least keep him locked away for an hour or two. Hopefully, the next time we spoke, I would have a big plate of crow to serve him.

"Any of you happen to know how to fight a demon?" I asked the assembled crowd. I received blank stares as a response. "Okay, then what good are you to me on this?"

I almost winced as the words came out. It wasn't exactly what I'd wanted to say, and the tone was totally wrong.

"We will die instead of you," Nose Wart said simply.

"How does that help?" I sputtered. I guess I shouldn't be surprised at an answer like that, but to hear it spoken so matter-of-factly was uncomfortable. Mostly because I knew that he was being very literal.

"We will throw ourselves at this demon until you have it under control. Those who die will become hallowed names in the tribe. Those of us that survive will honor them for the rest of our existence…and you will still be alive."

"Is it dark enough to move out?" I asked, deciding that any more questions about this subject were pointless.

"I believe that it is, miss," a voice said from the stairs.

I spun and staggered back a few steps. "Aoife…but you…you're…" I was suddenly struck with the total inability to form a sentence or complete a full thought.

"Am standing here wondering what sorts of things I have missed in my absence, miss." The siren walked down the steps the rest of the way and I was struck by how she had changed during her time away. "I have heard the song, and I am home where I belong if you will have me."

The Aoife that left me was barely able to pass for a girl in her mid-to-late teens. This version looked to be a twenty-something woman. She was still elegantly beautiful, her purple eyes shining as bright as ever, but she now had a womanlier body. Her curves were more…dangerous? Having a baby had done her right.

The baby! Something about her disappearing with the baby popped a bubble in my consciousness. She'd had a male child and was supposed to have taken it to the ocean and drown it. It was something between witches and sirens and I'm sure I don't know even a sliver of the story behind it.

"Lady Aoife," Nose Wart said with a reverence that he normally reserved for only me. "Welcome home. Your beauty and soothing voice has been missed. I do hope that you will offer a song over the bodies of those who fall in this coming battle."

The siren looked over at Nose Wart and then curtsied! Since when did she do that?

"Chief Nose Wart of the Just Goblin clan, it will be my honor to sing over the fallen…provided I am not among them when all is said and done." Aoife faced all the goblins who had gone totally still in a way that was very un-goblin-like. They were all staring with the same open-mouthed amazement like none of them had ever seen a woman before.

"Wait, excuse me?" I blurted once I realized what she had just said. "You're coming with us? Do you have any idea what we are about to do? And...not to be rude, but don't you have a baby?" I craned my neck to look past her like I expected the child to perhaps be in a stroller in the hallway or something.

"My child will be safe. He is with the nearby faeries," Aoife replied with a wave of her hand like it was of no consequence.

At least now I had some idea of how she was so up to date with the current situation. In fact, she was walking in with perhaps as much if not more of an idea than my little goblin hit squad.

"I've missed you so much," I blurted.

"And I have missed you as well." She gave me a smile that made me feel warm inside. "And we will have time to catch up on the things I have missed when we return. I would not suggest we go in to confront a demon with our minds distracted. They are a terribly powerful creature and could do all of us great harm."

Well, when she said it like that...

"What about me?" a voice said from the top of the stairs.

Aoife spun and I saw a soft silvery glow pulse from her skin. I have no idea where it came from, but she was suddenly holding a long, slender blade in her hands that looked like it was made of glass. It was only about two feet long, but the handle and guard were ornately carved stone that I am pretty sure is jade.

"Who are you?" Aoife hissed as she stepped between me and Colt who was frozen in his tracks like a deer in the headlights.

"Umm...Colt Faber?" He'd been so startled that it came out sounding like a question.

"You are a ghoul." Aoife glided across the room and stopped at the bottom of the stairs. "If you are here to challenge my mistress, I can assure you that you will have many battles to fight before you ever reach her."

"Umm, he's with me," I said as I came up beside the siren and placed a hand on her shoulder.

"Are you a mated pair?" Aoife spun to me with an expression of amusement on her face.

"No, but he is living here while he gets his feet underneath him."

"Where else would they be?" Now she looked confused and shot a quick glance at Colt to look him up and down as if she expected to discover that he was malformed.

"Morgan has him here so he can learn his function."

At the name of the Psychic, Aoife spun. "So you did not kill her?"

"What would make you think that?"

"I heard that you defeated a Psychic. I already knew that it was not Blumegastrickfiggernilly. A pair of witches on the island work for that disgusting little pig."

"Don't hold back, tell us how you really feel," I snorted.

"I believe that Blumegastrickfiggernilly should have his reproductive organs separated from the rest of his body," Aoife said matter-of-factly. "But since it wasn't him, I just assumed that you and Morgan finally parted ways."

"Then why would you think that I killed her?"

"Because no Psychic in their right mind would allow a female ghoul to slip from their grasp. If they did not have you in their district, then they would want you dead."

"Well it wasn't Morgan." I gave her a very brief rundown of my trip to Texas.

"We do *have* a lot to catch up on, miss," Aoife said with a hint of laughter in her voice.

"Yeah, well, we need to get going and take down this succubus, then we can sit down and catch up. I have a feeling that you have more than a few things to tell me as well."

I started up the stairs and stopped when I came to Colt who had not moved from the top of the landing. He folded his arms across his chest and regarded me with an arched eyebrow.

"What?" I stopped when it was clear that he wasn't going to move out of the way.

"There has to be something I can do. How can I help?" Colt asked.

"Yeah," I let that word draw out like the Bill Lumbergh character in that movie *Office Space*. "You see, this is kind of a big deal. I don't really think you are ready for it."

"Sounds to me like neither are you," he shot back.

He had a point, not that I would openly admit it and give him a reason to allow that smug look starting to grow on his face to gain more traction. "How many Supes have you had to fight so far?" I asked with just a hint of attitude.

"Gotta start someplace." He gave a shrug. "I'm sure you had to start someplace. Right?"

"It sure as hell wasn't with a freaking demon!"

"I'm a big boy, I am pretty sure I can handle my business."

I didn't have time to argue right now. A part of me wanted to insist that Colt stay behind, but at the same time, I'd already seen that I was out of my league when it came to fighting this thing alone.

"You can come, but you will need to do exactly what I say." The only problem now was that I really didn't have the slightest clue what I was going to do once I confronted the she-devil. I think I just said that because it seems to be what people in charge always say in those action flicks.

We all headed for the door, and I was just about to open it when Sexy Sadie piped up. "We have visitors approaching in the driveway."

"You wouldn't by chance be able to tell me who it is," I said to the air.

"Return visitors. Human. Three men from the group *Appetite for Deception*," Sexy Sadie purred.

I paused, glanced at Aoife and decided that she looked human enough to avoid suspicion. Whatever it was that these guys wanted, they were gonna have to make it quick or they were gonna lose any chance of getting their singer back.

"Hello, boys," I said as I opened the door right before Izzy was about to knock. BC Slash and Sorum were right behind him and had grim looks on their faces. It was not an expression that looked comfortable on BC's face.

"Hey, Ava," Izzy said with his usual casual demeanor. "Yeah, umm, we have a problem."

13

Back to the Front

"Can it wait? I have someplace that I have to be."

"I don't think so." The man tucked his hands into the rear pockets of his black jeans. "It's about Duff."

If he was possessed again I was going to cut his head off and worry about the consequences later. Now was not the time for Duff to do anything stupid, and I thought I'd made it clear that he was to just stay put until things were dealt with.

"He said he had an idea where Axl might be. He said he was going to 'prove his worth' to you and Rock for whatever that means. He also said that if he wasn't back within the hour, we should probably tell you."

"And I am assuming that it has been an hour," I said more to myself that Izzy.

"Oh yes…" Sorum got a bit pink in the face and I could see the other two suddenly looking away, hints of their own embarrassment visible on their cheeks and the tops of their ears. "Well, we were at the pizza place right down the street and sort of lost track of time. Izzy was sharing his new favorite pizza with me. Pepperoni, jalapeño cheese and smoked oysters."

"And I fell asleep," BC Slash offered.

"Okay," I said as evenly as possible, "how long has it been?"

The trio looked back and forth between each other. At last, it was Izzy who answered. "Almost three hours?"

Part of me wanted to slap each of them. Did they have any idea what they might've consigned their fellow band member and supposed friend to by leaving him in the clutches of a succubus? Yeah...well I didn't either, but I bet it's bad.

"Alright, I am going to go find your friends. I want you to stay here. Is that understood?" I made it a point to lock eyes with each of them until I got a nod or verbal affirmation.

"Is your friend going?" I turned to find BC eyeing Aoife up and down like she was a fresh water spring he'd just discovered in the middle of the desert. I doubted BC had ever gone thirsty a day in his adult life.

"She is," I answered, stepping into his field of vision. "And you aren't." That answer had a double-meaning that I'm certain went over BC Slash's head, but I didn't have any more time to waste. I turned to Colt. "You and Nose Wart go grab my gear that I have ready downstairs."

The two took off for the lower level leaving me and Aoife alone with three-fifths of *Appetite for Deception*. At any other time, I was willing to bet it would be a thrill to have such amazing musicians who obviously love at least some of the same music that I do standing around in my living room. Right now, it was just a pain in the butt.

I turned back to see Izzy and Sorum peering around in Colt's general direction and mentally slapped myself in the forehead. If I wasn't careful, I was going to have to kill the entire band before the night was over. My—and by that I actually mean their—only hope was that they would continue to demonstrate the same degree of obliviousness they'd shown from the start.

"We haven't met," I heard BC Slash whisper to Aoife. "I'm BC Slash. What's your name?"

"Aoife," the siren answered with just a hint of curtness in her tone.

There was a long pause. "Wow, that's a new one. Never

heard that name before. Where is it from?"

"My mother." And with that, the siren gave me a thin-lipped smile and headed out the front door with Nose Wart and Colt. I sighed and followed, wondering if I might be rubbing off on the normally sweet siren. I heard somebody's phone ring as I shut the door behind me. What sounded like Izzy calling after me was quickly silenced as I shut the door.

A few minutes later my motley team and I were at the way-point travel portal. Rain and a contingent of faeries stood with her. To anybody at any other time, this looked like nothing more than an etched design carved into the wall that depicted a wood-ed scene with trees, shrubs, and even dangling vines. The craftsmanship was so incredible that you almost swore that it was a real scene that somehow lacked any color other than the slate gray of the wall it had been carved into.

"You must stay on the green path. It will take you to your destination," Rain said as she began to touch and fondle some of the carved leaves, pine cones, and stones.

At last, she ran her hand down the length of the trunk of what I think was an oak tree and said something in a language that I didn't understand. As soon as she did, the scene trans-formed into a wall of mist. I stared at it and then back to Rain.

"Step through, Ava," the faerie godmother said coolly. "You must be the first in and the last out. It will close behind you on its own and open at your destination, so there is nothing else that you need do save return home with my people." She looked at me and then started before adding, "And the human...of course."

Something told me that Rain and I would be butting heads on this in a more powerful way before all was said and done. Luckily for her, I did not have a moment to spare. While the stroke of midnight was still hours away, time has a funny way of slipping through your fingers when you want it to last just as it can drag on forever when you want it to hurry.

The waypoint path supposedly originates from the heart of every Sidhe and will allow those who travel it to make a journey of up to hundreds of miles in mere minutes. Don't ask me about the magic that operates it because I haven't asked and I doubt that I would be told if I did.

There were paths of all colors and I stepped onto the green one. A soon as I did, all the others seemed to vanish. The route was lit with a dim glow that radiated from the walls, ceiling, and floor. I wasn't sure about how everyone else's vision worked but for me everything was crystal clear.

The path went straight and twice we passed intersections where other colored paths sprouted of in several directions. We stayed the course until we came to what I first thought was a dead end. But as soon as we were within about twenty feet, the wall turned to a thick mist and I ushered my team through before stepping out myself. I was only a little surprised when I stepped out and discovered that my exit "door" was the base of a giant oak tree.

"Everybody try to remember where this is," I said.

My reasoning was that just in case my fight with the succubus ended with us running for our lives (with or without Duff and Axl), I didn't want to be reenacting that same ritual I go through every time I park my car in the mall parking lot. You know, the one where you swear you parked in this one spot, yet you end up finding your car five rows over and seven spaces back.

Nose Wart stepped up beside me with a female goblin. She had what looked like a relatively fresh bite taken from one arm. "Toe Rot has perfect recall of the location."

The female goblin bowed low. "I will not fail you, Just Ava."

I didn't want to state the obvious that she would probably now end up being the first to die. Instead, I just gave a nod. The taste of ash and sulfur was strong again and I felt a tingle in my head that almost made me want to sneeze.

Hmm, that's new.

"There's something wrong," Colt whispered.

"What do you mean wrong?" I turned to him as he went full ghoul. His reply was little more than a series of frustrated sounds through his own Sharkmouth.

On the plus side, I heard it just seconds later. I turned as three individuals emerged from the trees to our left. A heartbeat after that, two more emerged from the right.

Templars.

"How fortunate," one of them said. He was a big man, skin so black that it almost looked purple as he stood in the shadows created by the canopy of trees above us. Even with my perfect night vision, he still almost blended into the darkness.

"I don't have time for this," I snarled.

"This won't take long." The man brought up an arm. He was holding one of those cursed ray guns.

There was a sudden screech and a trio of goblins rushed the man with a variety of wicked looking weapons. One of them looked almost like a giant potato peeler. Leading the charge, no surprise, was the female that would supposedly be able to bring us back to the waypoint without a hitch. I only knew it was her because I'd noticed the bite-sized chunk missing from her left arm.

The distraction was enough for the Templar to glance away from me for a split second. I took that opportunity to leap into the air as my switch fingers and toes sprang out. I landed with all twenty digits plunging into my would-be attacker. With a flick of the wrist I ripped his throat out. I am pretty sure I heard moans of disappointment from the goblins as they arrived a few heartbeats later.

I don't know what they were so upset about, there were still four remaining. The sounds of battle erupted and I did a quick scan to see if any of the others had one of the ray guns. All I saw were a variety of blades including a sword that glowed.

Colt flew past me and slammed into the next closest Templar looking more like a linebacker than a quarterback as he struck squarely with his shoulder into the man's chest, his head ducking to the side in a textbook tackle that could've been used in an instructional video.

That left three including the woman with the glowing blade. She was backed against a tree with four goblins dancing in and out as she jabbed and swiped. I faced off with the third man on

151

this side of the trail where we'd been ambushed. I had to be confident that the rest of my goblins would take out the fifth Templar.

"I look forward to making you watch as I feast on your useless milk bags, you smelly discharge from a sow's pee hole."

Ah, there was the Nose Wart I knew and loved. I briefly wondered if there was some special class that goblins attended to learn to insult or if it was just part of their genetics. Seriously, Don Rickles had nothing on these guys. (Rest in Peace, Mister Potato Head.)

I faced my opponent and saw his eyes flick to the ray gun. I promptly put myself between him and it. "Do you think you stand a chance in hell of surviving? Even if you defeat us—"

"No 'ifs' about it, stud. This fight was over the moment you stepped out of the trees," I cut the Templar off and actually felt pretty good about that retort. It wasn't all that witty but it conveyed just the right amount of cockiness.

The Templar didn't seem the least bit concerned or impressed as he pulled a blade from a sheath at his thigh and came at me in a low crouch. I was a little bit impressed seeing as how he didn't rush me. This was a fighter who knew how what he was doing.

As the other battles raged on around me, my opponent and I circled one another. Each of us feinted in and out a few times to test the other, but neither were eager to over-commit.

Slay him and feast on his carcass, a voice in my head screamed. It sounded like it was coming from down a long, padded hallway. I'll give you three guesses as to who that was and the first two don't count.

I wanted to ensure my locks were in place but I didn't dare take my attention from my opponent. I had no idea what sort of weapon I was facing but I was willing to bet that it was designed just especially for me. Sorta like that Grand Prize they used to give away on the old *Newlywed Game* with Bob Eubanks. You know…the show where married couples try to guess what the other might say and actually had one woman answer the question: Where is the strangest place you've made whoopee? To which she answered, "In the butt, Bob."

I jumped back from another slashing attack with the weapon and saw a chance to counter with both hands. I attempted my best *Predator* impersonation and slashed outward. That proved to be the wrong move. My opponent had lured me in and was ready for me. He dove under my attack and came up with a thrust that would've skewered my heart and killed me if my heart was still a vital organ. I was already searching for something to block the pain I was certain had to be coming.

His face melted from its triumphant grin to a look of confusion with just a hint of resignation. Yeah, he knew what was coming next. I drove the switch fingers of my right hand through his neck and lopped off his head. Wow, there is A LOT of blood in a human body. He fell back and I glanced down at his blade, mildly confused as to why it seemed to have no effect on me. I could puzzle over that later, I decided.

Just to be on the safe side, I popped the severed head into my mouth and spun to see who could use my help. I was just in time to see Colt stand up, bend over, and retch like a cat hacking up a hairball. Only, in his case, it was the clothing his opponent had been wearing.

Not even one of my goblins had fallen in the battle. I did a quick scan and saw that everybody on my side of the little fight was still standing.

I could not hear anything else coming our direction and did a fast scan to try and get a finer tuned location of the succubus. The pain and the taste in my throat increased when I oriented myself on a thick grove of trees just ahead and slightly to the right.

I started in that direction and began doing something most people would say is impossible…I did two things at once. I simultaneously redoubled my securing of Boudicca, and began to let the song *Let Me Go to the Show* by Poison start on a loop in my head. Almost instantly the pain lessened. As an added bonus, the sulfur and ash taste faded to the point where it was almost manageable.

It didn't take long to locate Jillea the succubus. And, big surprise, both Mark and Duff were with her along with a handful of male faeries. They all had blank, glassy looks on their faces except for Duff. He looked like he might be in pain. I gave a sniff and didn't detect anything troublesome beyond the normal human death rate.

"Look who came to play," Jillea said as she spread her bat-like wings and rose just a few feet off the ground. "I guess I underestimated you."

"Don't beat yourself up over it," I said with a dismissive wave of one hand while walking fully into the clearing where she'd hidden to wait for midnight. "You aren't the first and I doubt you'll be the last."

"Hmm," Jillea pinched her lower lip and gave her head a small shake, "actually, I think I might be." She paused and then added, "The last to underestimate you that is."

"You really think word will get out that I kicked your slutty behind back to wherever you came from and that other beasties will start taking me seriously?" I asked with mock enthusiasm.

The succubus scowled. Twice she opened her mouth only to shut it again.

"Oh, miss, you really are getting better at this," Aoife said sweetly as she took her place on my left shoulder while Colt stepped up beside me on the right. The goblins all eased between or around us and formed a wall of snarling menace that Jillea did not appear to even notice.

"I'm feeling generous," I said, bolstered not only by my little contingent but also by Aoife's appraisal. "I am going to let you return to your plane. Now, before you answer," I spoke quickly when she started to retort, "I'm going to insist that you leave the humans and faeries behind. But on the plus side, I understand that being actually banished from this place due to losing in combat will confine you to your own plane for a very long time."

"And where would you hear such lies?" Jillea scoffed. "Those rules only apply to the major demons."

154

Her goat eyes blinked and I saw her black, forked tongue make a swipe across her perfect lips. For all the icky things like the tail, bat wings, and goat eyes, she was still amazingly beautiful. Yet, despite her peculiarities, I knew the signs of deception when I saw them. She was almost textbook in her tells. If she broke out into a sweat, that would be the clincher.

"Okay, if you aren't willing to just give them over freely, then you leave me with no choice."

I took a step forward and instantly found myself in total darkness. I froze for just a moment and then allowed the pain and taste cues to help me orient on her. She'd very smartly moved several feet to the right.

"Just Ava?" Nose Wart hissed. "I can't see."

Grumbles of agreement came from the other goblins. I heard something that sounded like the yelp one would let loose with if they stubbed their toe which was quickly followed by a muttered curse from a female goblin.

"Have no worries, miss," Aoife said calmly. A moment later, she began a soft tune that pushed the blackness away much like the sunrise does the night each morning.

"A siren," Jillea squealed, clapping her hands. "Her essence will sustain me for months…perhaps years."

"Don't count your chickens," I spat as I took the opportunity to leap forward and place myself just a few feet from the succubus while effectively shielding the bodies of Axl and Duff from her.

The look on Jillea's face was priceless. She looked around at her feet and it took me a moment to realize that she was actually looking for chickens.

I decided to take that moment to launch myself at the succubus with all my claws aimed at her middle. The pain in my head tried to shove aside my musical distraction at the moment in the song where Bobby Dall screamed, "You heard your mother, turn that shit off!"

That was also the same instance when Jillea blinked out of existence with an audible pop that sounded like somebody squeezing a sheet of bubble wrap. I slammed into the concrete wall of af a small shed that the rusting sign on the door declared was the property of the Department of Portland Water Works.

It didn't hurt, but it did jar me just a bit. I turned as Colt dropped his shoulder and tried to plow into the demon from behind. She vanished again and then re-appeared. But either she was now going on the offensive, or she miscalculated. Whatever the case, she appeared in the midst of the goblins who wasted no time setting on her in a frenzy of blades and bludgeons.

On the one hand, she did look very annoyed. Unfortunately, I could see no evidence on her body that the attacks were doing any damage. Not one nick, bruise, or even red mark appeared to indicate that the goblin's assault was doing the slightest harm.

Colt was getting up when the succubus leveled both her hands, palms out, in his direction. A crackle was accompanied by the smell of ozone as a bolt of electricity shot from her and slammed into his chest knocking him back against the concrete wall again.

This was another case of size not meaning a damn thing. He probably had her by a foot and maybe even as much as a hundred pounds.

She was not facing me directly and I hopped up and flew at her again. She didn't pop out this time but instead turned into mist which I flew through. I felt a chill coat my skin that went to my bones. I had not been exposed to any degree of heat or cold that had demonstrated the ability to have much effect on me up to that point. It was almost enough to frighten me.

Almost.

I hit the ground on my feet and spun to face Jillea. "Are we going to do this all night?"

"We can…at least until I depart. But I do believe that I will have to come back and play with you again, ghoul." Jillea eyed me with more of a look of hunger than amusement. "You might not possess an energy that I can feed from, but there must be some way I can bend your will and have you as my own."

I wasn't sure what to think about that statement. Was she going to be yet another to bid for my services and make ridiculous offers of wealth and power?

I opened my mouth to say something that I was sure would have been witty gold. Unfortunately, I would never know for sure. The sound of a car's engine registered to my ears. It was surprisingly close which told me the degree that I'd been concentrating up until that moment.

Jillea looked past me, her head cocked to the side and her eyes narrowed like she could see who had arrived and was not happy about it. Was it reinforcements for me? Or, and this seemed more likely, was it somebody or something that would work against me? Could it be more Templars?

"His phone is this way," a familiar voice called out.

It was Izzy. I gave a sniff and detected two others with him. That, and the smell of pepperoni pizza, garlic, sardines…and mint? I had no idea what Izzy and Sorum were snacking on, but I was certain that not only would I find both of them eating, but that whatever it was, it would be "grody to the max," to quote Moon Unit Zappa. And seriously, do I have to say it?

Jillea's body tensed and her wings fluttered just a bit. She tucked into a crouch and looked to be getting ready to launch herself into the air.

In that split second of distraction, apparently the goblins, Aoife, and I all had the same thought. The siren broke into a song as the goblins all rushed with a chorus of howls and shrieks that were a jumbled mass of curses combined with war whoops and I leapt once more with hands and feet aimed at my foe.

The succubus had just enough time to utter a strange word and fling a hand out in our direction. The ground rumbled just a bit and then began to open in spots. What appeared to be a variety of cats, dogs, and…squirrels—yep, those were squirrels—crawled out from the earth. It didn't take a genius to see that most of these things had been dead for a long time.

I slammed into the succubus and we tumbled end over end, a nest of tangled arms, legs, and bat wings. Unfortunately we ended up with her on top. She looked down at me and snarled, her canine teeth looking very similar to those of a vampire's.

"You will pay for that, bitch," Jillea hissed.

157

And then we were piled on by my little band of goblins. Nose Wart scrambled atop Jillea's head and grabbed two fists full of hair, yanking back for all he was worth. Without even batting an eye, the succubus reached back, snatched him free, losing two good clumps of hair in the process. She then flung my little goblin friend at a tree where he hit with an ugly sounding crunch and fell to the ground in a heap.

"NO!" I screamed, and plunged my switch fingers into the meaty breasts that had been barely contained by what looked and felt like black leather.

Jillea howled, letting me know that I'd hurt her. That was enough to give me room to buck her forward and off of me. I rolled over and came up to my hands and knees prepared to at-tack. A female goblin beat me to it and threw herself onto the succubus' back, right between her bat wings.

I unslung the pouch I'd used to carry the Dead Sea sea salt in and poured out a circle around us. As soon as I connected the circle, I shouted, "*Luuke panda!*"

There was a metallic pinging sound and then a shimmery globe of energy sprang up around us. That was the same moment that Izzy, Sorum, and BC burst through the branches and arrived in our little clearing.

"Whoa!" Sorum breathed, taking a bite from whatever it was that he had wrapped up in greasy looking brown paper.

I felt my heart sink at the idea that I might be forced to kill the entire band at this point. All my efforts had just fallen apart. There was no way that I could explain any if this away. It almost would've been easier to let Jillea have Axl and Duff.

Then I heard Aoife's song change to something that would make Enya jealous. All three men froze, their expressions going blank. Sorum even dropped whatever it was he'd been eating, and when his mouth fell open, the partially chewed food tumbled down his chin and onto the grass at his feet.

Jillea flipped onto her back, apparently trying to crush the goblin as she bucked wildly, smashing her hips down hard over and over. I had to use this opportunity before she could direct her attention back to me. I grabbed the canister of silver ash, popped the top, and seasoned the succubus liberally with the dust as I hummed along with Tony Bennet as he appeared at random in my head to tell me how he'd left his heart in San Francisco.

"*Wanya rauko.*"

No sooner had I said the words when a wind started to swirl. The thing was, it only looked to be happening inside my circle. Jillea's head snapped up and her eyes went wide.

"No, this is not possible," she wailed, sounding a lot like the Wicked Witch in *The Wizard of Oz.* "Curse you, ghoul, to the core of your being. And know this…when you die, I will be waiting, and I shall see personally to your torment."

The wind amped up and a tornado of dirt, dead leaves, and a few partially decomposing rodents whipped around inside my circle. I flinched and had to crouch low to stay clear of everything.

There was an overwhelming stench of sulfur and I swear I could see something in the cyclone. It looked as if a portal to some other world had opened. Two red eyes stared out through swirling smoke and gouts of flame as black hands reached out and grasped the succubus. And then I saw the tiny figure on Jillea's back. The goblin was still there!

I opened my mouth, but no words came. I'd done it again. I'd killed another of Nose Wart's women. Sure, there hadn't been any announcement that he'd chosen Toe Rot, but I'd seen the bites. They'd already done the taste test.

A roar came from that portal along with a scream. I saw Jillea fly backwards into the portal, her body bending back at an impossible angle for any spine to endure. Just before the portal winked shut, I caught a glimpse of the goblin. Maybe it was my brain trying to make it easier for me to endure, but her expression was very much like a child riding on one of those coin-operated ponies that used to be found in front of grocery stores.

Just as suddenly as it had begun, the wind stopped and everything settled. Looking around, I saw that the undead varmints had deactivated like puppets with their strings cut. Bones and bits fell to the ground just as lifeless as they'd been moments before. Aoife was still singing and a glow encompassed her and the other three members of *Appetite for Deception*. She gave me a smile and nodded as if to let me know that everything was fine on her end.

I looked over to where I'd seen Axl, Duff, and the male faeries clustered when we'd arrived. They were still there, each of them blinking his eyes and looking around in confusion.

I stood, running the toe of my boot through the salt circle like I'd seen Rock do. The force field or whatever it was vanished with a sizzle and a hint of ozone.

I counted my goblins and saw that seven of them still stood. All in all, we hadn't suffered much in the way of casualties. Of course there was still the matter of what I would do with the members of *Appetite*, but that would have to come later.

I started across the clearing to where I'd seen Nose Wart thrown. It was at that moment that I realized he could very well be a casualty. If that was the case, then this had been a total disaster. It might seem callous, but I would gladly trade all five members of the band for my little goblin friend.

A pair of female goblins were kneeling beside a figure sprawled at the base of the tree where Nose Wart had been hurled. I shoved them aside and swear I heard one of them growl at me. Well, I would deal with that later, right now, my only focus was on the unmoving form of the chieftain of the Just Goblin clan.

"Nose Wart?" My voice sounded weak and scared in my own ears. I placed my hand on his chest and leaned forward to sniff him.

A jagged and pitted blade was suddenly at my throat. "You will not feed on our chief," a goblin voice warned.

I turned my head to see an ugly face made even worse by the sneering and curled lips that were peeled back to show teeth that had never known a dentist...or a toothbrush. I shot a look at the blade and then looked back into the goblin's eyes.

"Get that thing away from me or I will use it to carve out

your own heart which I will eat before that tiny brain in your hideous head has the chance to remind you that you are dead."

"You have learned nothing of how to properly curse." My head snapped down to the body of Nose Wart to see his eyes partially opened. "And you forgot to spit."

"Nose Wart!" I scooped the goblin into my arms. There was a pained grunt as I squeezed him to me.

"Please set me down, Just Ava," Nose Wart coughed, his voice muffled from his face being smashed into my breasts.

"Sorry." I eased him away and back to the ground.

"Toe Rot," Nose Wart groaned.

I was about to start an apology that was feeling like a habit when the voice of the goblin that had been holding a blade to my throat stepped past me and knelt beside the injured chief of my special clan. "I am here, my mate and giver of the seed that will grow our clan into a force that none will wish to see on the battlefield."

I sat back on my rear, a feeling of relief washing through me. I looked over at Aoife and saw that her glow had taken in Axl and Duff. The male faeries were now apparently back in control of their minds and had assembled in a row just behind the siren.

"You have defeated the succubus, miss." She flashed me a smile.

"Yeah, but she might've gotten away with it if it weren't for those meddling kids," I said as I nodded to the members of *Appetite for Deception*."

"Shall I wipe their minds?"

"You can do that?"

Aoife nodded. "It is a simple glamour. At most, they would think this nothing more than a dream."

"Then do it."

Aoife's song changed again and all five members of the band sank to the ground in a heap. After a moment, the siren stopped her song and gave a nod of satisfaction. "They will wake feeling refreshed and with no memory of the past few days."

161

"So basically like any other rock band after a show and a crazy night of partying," I mumbled.

Ten minutes later, we were travelling along the magic path with two of the faeries carrying Nose Wart on a hastily made litter constructed from one of their capes and a pair of fallen tree limbs. Colt seemed no worse for wear but he refused to make eye contact with me and kept his distance. And then we were home.

There was a big fuss as Rain and some of her people saw her men step through the waygate. Toe Rot called for the goblins to come and transport their leader to his room. Aoife waved them away, insisting that she carry him personally. Colt stalked off without a word making me think that we were probably right back where we'd started before this whole ordeal.

For some reason, I didn't feel like hanging around. My mind was stuck on the fact that I'd sent some poor goblin to the Abyss or wherever demons come from. Race was captive someplace. The voices in my head were not any of the ones I counted on or needed. Sure, to some, it could feel like a happy ending. But for me, I had a feeling that things were just getting warmed up…and the worst was yet to come.

***

"Do you know where you are?" Axl M screamed over the rhythmic guitar intro.

I stood in the rear of the room. Rock was to my left and Aoife on my right. The crowd erupted in response to Axl M's words. I'd seen what I came to see. The band seemed fully re-covered, and we'd crossed paths before the show. Most of them never even glanced my direction; although BC Slash did give Aoife a good look. I doubt Izzy or Sorum could see anything past the giant hero sandwiches that they were chomping on.

The only one who'd made direct eye contact with me (and yes, I have my dark shades on) was Duff. I might've imagined it, but I could've sworn that he winked at me and gave a slight nod of his head. Rock hadn't said anything, so I dismissed it.

Of course, I'd come to this show with a purpose other than to see if Aoife's forget spell worked. For one, this was probably the last night of peace I would have for a while. There had been no word in the past several days from the people who had Race and Rock said that she wanted to be proactive instead of waiting for them to make the next move.

We were going to start with a few of the lower level flunkies that she knew stood against us. Hopefully we would be able to get them to spill the beans on where my man was being kept. But I seriously doubted it would be that easy.

My head has been silent for this past week. Maybe I finally got Mystify locked down tight, or maybe he just didn't feel the need to bother me. The more disturbing silence came from Boudicca. Even locked away, I at least felt...something. But ever since the battle with the succubus, I hadn't felt anything.

Appetite for Deception finished their set and I felt a tingle in my belly. I watched as the crowd headed for the bar to get drinks before the next band hit the stage. A few waited by the side of the stage where the members of *Appetite* would eventually emerge to mingle.

"And this is what humans call music?" Aoife grumped from beside me. I glanced at her. "There is nothing musical about that noise."

"Don't be such an old lady." I gave her a playful elbow.

I felt a tap on the shoulder and turned to see that Duff had somehow crept up behind me. "Thanks for coming out tonight," he said.

I opened my mouth and shut it a few times as I found myself at a loss. I was still trying to decide if he was being polite and that this was just a coincidence when he brought up his left hand and flashed a familiar ring.

"Rock didn't tell you?" I shook my head. "Yeah, she agreed to bring me on as her plebe."

"And you didn't think to say anything?" I turned to the Templar.

"Surprise?" the large woman said with a weak smile. "So

maybe now is the wrong time to ask if he can stay at your place while we are gone? I was sorta hoping that Theodre could give him a few history lessons while we are out of town."

I was about to say something snarky when the house lights dimmed and the next band hit the stage. I looked up and all my annoyance drained from my body.

"Ladies and gentlemen...make some noise for *Poison'us!*"

The stage was flooded in greens and pinks. My eyes locked on the man who grabbed the microphone stand in the center of the stage. He was beautiful.

There was a war about to start. I was going to have to kill or be killed. It was very probable that I would lose friends over the next however long this war took. Hell, I might lose the man I loved before it even started. Tonight might be the last time for a while that I could enjoy myself.

As the band tore into the song "Talk Dirty to Me" I let all my worries and anxiety slip away. I melted into the music. My eyes never left the singer for a moment. I was going to savor every second.

Step into the DEAD world created by TW Brown -
Follow along with the DEAD - the 12 book series starting with
The Ugly Beginning - or enjoy a few laughs following Ava
Birch's adventures in the horror/comedy That Ghoul Ava

MAY DECEMBER
Publications

**The growing voice in horror
and speculative fiction.**

Find us at www.maydecemberpublications.com
Or
Email us at contact@maydecemberpublications.com

TW Brown is the author of the ***Zomblog*** series, his horror comedy romp, ***That Ghoul Ava***, and, of course, the ***DEAD*** series. Safely tucked away in the beautiful Pacific Northwest, he moves away from his desk only at the urging of his Border Collie, Aoife. (Pronounced Eye-fa)

He plays a little guitar on the side...just for fun...and makes up any excuse to either go trail hiking or strolling along his favorite place...Cannon Beach. He answers all his emails sent to twbrown.maydecpub @gmail.com and tries to thank everybody personally when they take the time to leave a review of one of his works.

His blog can be found at:http://twbrown.blogspot.com

The best way to find everything he has out is to start at his Author Page:

You can follow him on twitter @maydecpub and on Facebook under Todd Brown, Author TW Brown, and also under May December Publications.

www.ingramcontent.com/pod-product-compliance
Lightning Source LLC
Chambersburg PA
CBHW071246130626
46556CB00003B/1184